Praises for
ARIZONA GHOST STORIES
by Antonio R. Garcez

"ARIZONA GHOST STORIES gives a hauntingly accurate overview to the many reports of haunted sites all over the state. It not only lists the places from north to south but quotes the interviews of eyewitnesses giving a remarkable feeling of being there with them as they encounter the unknown. Such sites as the Copper Queen Hotel in Bisbee to the Jerome Inn come to life in Mr. Garcez's investigations. His chapter on the reports of ghosts at Tombstone is perhaps one of the best accounts I have seen on this subject."

—Richard Senate

"The accounts range from sweetly sentimental to truly terrifying, but all share the benefit of Antionio's sensitivity and attention to detail. He shows respect for the tales, and those who tell them, and understands that history and culture are inexticably bound to all folklore."

—Jo-Anne Christensen

"Arizona could not have asked for a better chronicler of its supernatural landscape than Antonio R. Garcez. From Arivaca to Yuma, Arizona's most haunted places are all here! These stories will send shivers up your spine, and rightly so—they all really took place! If you ever wanted to experience something paranormal, let this book be your guide!"

—Dennis William Hauck

"These are not long-ago cowboy yarns, but very real, very current ghost stories from a rich and chilling mix of voices. Antonio has a rare talent for the telling detail; he paints unforgettably creepy images that linger long after the book is done."

—Chris Woodyard

"The reader is transported into the world of the supernatural, by a great storyteller who weaves history and personal interviews into a series of riviting tales, sure to make your skin crawl! Here, restless spirits of the past meet present-day skeptics head on. Memories come to life in the stories from 19 diverse Arizona counties. The thoughtfully told, well-researched stories are sometimes frightening, oftentimes chilling, and always fascinating."

—Rob & Anne Wlodarski

Praises for
THE ADOBE ANGELS GHOST BOOK SERIES OF NEW MEXICO BY ANTONIO R. GARCEZ

This collection of personal encounters with the 'spiritual' or 'supernatural' certainly supported some of my own experiences. These stories are made more frightening by their very proximity.
—*Stephanie Gonzales, NM Secretary of State*

I highly recommend that both local citizens and visitors to Santa Fe read this book!
—*Sam Pick, Mayor-Santa Fe, NM*

Fascinating to read, ADOBE ANGELS offers the reader insight into our town's unique traditions, folklore and history; don't miss it!
—*Frederick A. Peralta, Mayor-Town of Taos*

Important documentation of the people and history of northern New Mexico. Keep writing!
—*Kathleen Knoth, Librarian, Millicent Rogers Museum, Taos NM*

At last someone has written a book about the ghost tales people have been telling here for years!
—*Tom Sharpe, Albuquerque Journal*

It's enough to send shivers right up your spine! An excellent effort by Antonio Garcez and I anxiously await his next book!
—*Dale Kaczmarek, Ghost Research Society*

GOOD STUFF!—*Fortean Times Magazine, London, UK*

If you're a lover of the supernatural, get cozy in an easy chair and prepare your self for the inevitable. Eyewitness accounts told in a straightforward manner!
—*Tim Palmieri, Western Outlaw-Lawman History Association*

Another terrifying book from Garcez. I found this one even scarier than the first!
—*Chris Woodyard, Invisible Ink-Books on Ghosts & Hauntings*

Highly Entertaining!
—*Mary A. Sarber, Texas Book Columnist, El Paso, Herald-Post*

ADOBE ANGELS

ARIZONA

GHOST

STORIES

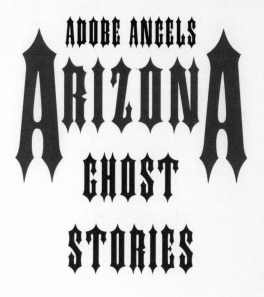

ADOBE ANGELS
ARIZONA
GHOST
STORIES

ANTONIO R. GARCEZ

RED RABBIT PRESS

Truth or Consequences, New Mexico

All photos were taken by the author, except where otherwise noted.
Cover photo by the author, cover & book design by
John Cole GRAPHIC DESIGNER, Santa Fe, New Mexico

First Edition

Printed in Canada

Library of Congress Catalog Card Number: 98-66351
ISBN Number: 0-9634029-5-1

To inquire about scheduling the author for public appearances,
you may write to the address below.

Published in 1998 by
Antonio R. Garcez
c/o Red Rabbit Press
P.O. Box 968
Truth or Consequences, NM 87901

DEDICATION

To my brother Vicente R. Garcez,
I will always be grateful.

Death is not a period but a comma in the story of life.

TABLE OF CONTENTS

PREFACE

This book, the fourth in my series about ghost books of the Southwest, has a two-fold purpose; first, I have researched and presented the very first book of Arizona ghost stories, and second, I hope to have introduced opened minds to the possibility that, with a bit of investigation and reflection, ghosts do exist.

I do not intend to have all the answers or to prove why ghosts exist, or why they present themselves to only certain individuals and not others. Attempts to provide explanations to those concepts have been presented over and over again by numerous other persons, both sincere and insincere. The fact remains that the living cannot define ghosts; ghosts control their own definitions!

As in my previous three books, on New Mexico ghosts, ghosts or spirits have always played recognized roles in family structures, and the arts-poetry, song, dance-of the American Indian and the Spanish-speaking. Are these two cultural groups more of a "target" for ghosts? Not likely. I believe simply that these groups, given their social and spiritual complexities, are more *sensitive* and accepting of the possibility that ghosts do exist. The traditions of burial rites, symbology, and belief in the duality of life and death are very much a part of their ceremonial observances. But they are not alone. Throughout history, one of the most insistent and deeply emotional human desires has been to know what becomes of us when we die. So many questions go unanswered, so many possibilities remain.

Even before recorded history, a universal experience of ghosts established itself in cultures, languages, and folklore throughout the world. Accounts that have passed the test of time remind us that the living have genuinely seen and been in direct contact with ghosts or spirits. The vast majority of these experiences are positive. Ghosts can be independent of the living, but the living cannot be independent of ghosts.

Through the research and investigation from all my books, I have come to recognize that making contact with a spirit or ghost is not at all that difficult. It is an extremely common phenomenon; contact may not just be *visual*. It may also be associated with hearing, a "feeling", smell and touch.

It is easy to overemphasize the negative aspects of ghosts as evil, scary, etc. However, focusing on these simplistic points alone promotes neither a positive nor hopeful view of our own end result. The best definitions of the existence of ghosts must be viewed through our own traditions. As I have said, I am inclined to believe that ghosts do exist and are manifest among us.

Antonio R. Garcez

ACKNOWLEDGEMENTS

My deepest appreciation to the following

Hank Estrada

Thanks to :

Arizona Department of Commerce—Don Harris, *Communications Director*, Mary Melendez, *Administrative Secretary*, for the use of each cities Community Profile and map.

Arizona State Parks—History of Yuma Territorial Prison, Picture of John Ryan.

Jerome Chamber of Commerce/Jerome Historical Society—History of Clinkscale building.

Yuma Department of Community Redevelopment/ Yuma Convention and Visitors Bureau-History of Yuma County Courthouse.

Robert Altherr—History of Jerome Grand Hotel.

Holbrook Chamber of Commerce/Historical Society of Navajo County (original documents held at Arizona State Archives, Department of Library Archives and Public Records)-Invitations to hanging of George Smiley and Deposition of T.J. McSweeny Steve and Gloria Goldstein—The Legend of "The Swamper," Craig H. Rothen—Photo of "Howard."

Albuquerque Rattlesnake Museum, New Mexico.

And my own personal thanks to the men, women and children of Arizona with HIV/AIDS and their care givers. You are all our teachers and truly our living angels. And especially to every person whom I interviewed for this book.

INTRODUCTION

Before deciding to write a book of Arizona ghost stories, I checked the usual sources to begin my research: libraries, bookstores, etc. I was genuinely surprised to discover that there were no books to be found on the subject. There were plenty of books on ghost towns and legends of the west, but no book devoted specifically to the *ghosts*. Amazing.

Given its particular wealth of land, culture, people, and unique history, I felt that the state of Arizona was long overdue for a collection of ghost stories. The stories of gunfighters, lovers, ranchers, miners, convicts, business owners, farmers, and American Indian points of view all are included in this book. Families, and friends we knew, spoke to, walked with, played with, who now lie under Arizona adobe soil are in this book. Men,women, and children who wait tirelessly for us in deser landscapes, houses, bars, hotels, and shaded avenues-they too are in this book.

These memories, come back to life, have come forth to re-enter our-world of the living. Men, women, and children who wait tirelessly for us in and among desert landscapes, houses, bars, hotels, and shaded avenues—they too are in this book.

You'll find them all within these pages-the murmuring voices; darting shadows; misty faces twisted in silent screams; empty, staring eyes of the wronged; angry booted footsteps of the condemned; and the vaporous svelte bodies of women with dark, empty eye sockets. They are all here.

Ghosts offer the living not only curious and sometimes terrifying fodder for stories and folklore, but also insight into another world in which time and space cease to exist. These samples of stories from Arizona provide readers with engaging reading and a bit of a history lesson as well.

Now relax, find a comfortable chair, fix yourself a strong pot of campfire coffee and prepare yourself for a long and bumpy ride into the realm of Arizona's ghosts. Remember, it's best not to keep your hosts waiting long, although they do have all the time in the world, they anger much too easily. Reservations are not required, because after all, your arrival has been pre-confirmed-far in advance!

Enjoy.

ARIVACA

Arivaca, about 11 miles north of Arizona's border with Mexico, was mapped by Father Eusebio Kino in 1695. It is in an area that contains some of the oldest mines in the United States. Arivaca, which is unincorporated, is about 56 miles southwest of Tucson in southern Pima county.

The locale may have been a Tohono O'odham (Pima) Indian village before 1751, when natives revolted against the Spanish, who were attracted by precious metals and excellent grazing land. Mines developed by the Spaniards were worked by Indians under the direction of Tumacacori Mission padres. In 1833, the Mexican government approved a petition by brothers Tomas and Ignacio Ortiz to raise cattle and horses on 8,677 acres of land that formed the Aribac Ranch. "OLa AribacO" is an Indian word meaning" small springs". Although boundaries for the ranch were never certain, its rights were bought by the Sonora Exploring and Mining Company in 1856. This company operated mines near Arivaca and Tubac. Also located on the ranch were reduction works for the Heintzelman Mine. The post office was established in 1878.

Charles Poston, Othe father of Arizona, O acquired the property in 1870 and later asked the U.S. government to confirm his right to 26,508 acres. The U.S. surveyor general recommended confirmation of 8,680 acres, but the U.S. Congress took no action. Poston's rights were obtained by the Arivaca Land and Cattle Company, which asked the U.S. Court of Private Land Claims to approve the land claim. The court refused, saying it was Oimpossible to identify...the land which was intended to be granted.O This decision was upheld by the U.S. Supreme Court on March 24, 1902, and the land became part of the public domain.

Arivaca now is primarily a retirement and residential area.

Frances Torres's Story

I interviewed Frances at her home in Arivaca, a small little town tucked within a quaint desert valley. Within this quiet town lies Frances's two-bedroom home. From the street, the house reveals no indication of what had transpired just a few years ago within its walls.

Frances preferred that I not describe the outside of her house; by doing so, some of her neighbors might know who she was and begin to gossip. Given her concern, I have chosen not to use her real name.

My story about "El Coyote" took place just a couple of years ago. I have made sure not to tell many people about what happened in the house because, being a small town, the gossip gets around really quickly.

I used to rent and live in the house next to the one I live in now. I used to know the old woman who was the owner of the property. When I moved into the house next door, she and I began to talk, and we became very friendly with each other. Some mornings she and I would have coffee in my kitchen. She sure was a talker. She told me about her son who lived in Tucson, and I got to meet him a few times before she died.

I recall that the first time I visited her, she showed me around the inside of her home. I noticed that one of her bedrooms had a door with nails hammered into the door frame. I asked her about this because it was very strange to have this door nailed shut the way it was. Hanging on one of the nails was a small metal crucifix. Her explanation was that she had nailed the door shut because of "El Coyote." I asked her, "Who was El Coyote?" She said he was a bad spirit that needed to be kept locked up. I thought to myself, "living by herself for so long made this old woman go nuts." I asked her why the spirit had the name of El Coyote. She said she had given it that name because although she had never really seen the spirit's face, its body looked like a wild dog. By this time, I thought to myself that this poor woman needed to get out of the house more often and mingle with people.

I didn't think much more about the "friend" she kept locked up in the bedroom. I never heard any loud noises coming from her home, and after all, she was really sweet. One day while she was at the post office, I walked to the rear of her house and looked inside the bedroom window where she kept El Coyote. I didn't know what I would expect to see.

Inside, I saw a room without any furniture. It didn't even have any rugs. "Poor old woman," I thought, " she must have invented this ghost as her own personal friend." I began to feel sorry for her because I myself have never married, and sometimes it does get lonely. But there wasn't anything unusual about the room, so I never mentioned it to her again.

Well, less than a year later, the woman spent Thanksgiving in Tucson with her son and his family. I know she was very happy because , after returning home, all she did was talk to me about how nice her visit had been.

Two days later, I paid her a visit to show her a large holiday greeting card that had arrived at my house. I knocked on her front door, and when she did not answer, I walked to the rear door, which was left unlocked, and walked inside. I immediately smelled gas. I took a few slow cautious steps into the house and kept calling her name. There was no answer. I got scared and quickly walked through the house. When I entered her bedroom, I found her lifeless body in bed. A flexible copper hose leading from the wall to her gas heater had developed a small hole.

After her funeral, her son told me that he was going to sell his mother's house. I asked him if he would sell it to me, and he agreed. I also asked him if he knew anything about the closed door that was nailed shut or about El Coyote. He said that his mother only mentioned "El Coyote" a few times but that he thought it was something crazy his mother had made up.

After I bought the house, two friends who lived in the town of Nogales, came to Arivaca to help me with repairs. I was overjoyed to finally own a house of my own. I began to remove old wallpaper and paint every inside wall. Of course, the first thing I did was to remove the nails on the bedroom door where "El Coyote" lived. During the repair work, I never noticed any strange noise or saw any ghost. Finally after a few weeks, the house was in move-in condition.

After moving all my belongings into the house, I soon began to notice that the rear bedroom was strangely very much colder than the rest of the house. At first I was not bothered by it, but then I began to wonder. Sometimes it was so cold that I got goose bumps on my arms. Other times, it was like stepping outside into a cool night. I thought about what the old woman had told me, but then I figured that my imagination was working overtime.

As the weeks passed, things began to get worse. Day and night

I began to see strange shadows in the house. I don't mean shadows shaped like a person,- they were more like a large blanket that covered the wall! One afternoon, I was washing dishes, and I heard a strange voice. Because I was in the kitchen, I had the volume on the TV in the living room turned up high, so that I could listen. I thought that perhaps the voice was coming from the television. I stopped washing the dishes because I felt a very strong feeling that someone was in the kitchen with me. I turned around to look behind me. I saw this huge black shadow—it covered the whole wall—move slowly then quickly across the room and into the hallway.

It couldn't have been the shadow of a passing car because the kitchen is located in the rear of the house. A passing plane couldn't have caused it either, because it would have to be flying level with the house. No, I immediately knew this was something that had to do with the spiritual world. Even though I was a bit shaken, I walked into the hallway and looked in the bathroom, closet, and the bedrooms. As soon as I entered the last bedroom, immediately the cold feeling came over me. I knew I had to get out of there fast!

I closed the door behind me and left it closed until the following week, when I had someone pay me a visit. I had ordered a pair of new closet doors. They were delivered by a Nogales contractor who carried the new doors off his truck and into the bedroom. Everything was going fine. I was in the living room watching television while the sound of his electric drill was making a loud noise. I remember walking to the bedroom and asking the contractor if he wanted some coffee. He said "no," and I left him alone to finish the job of installing the doors.

Suddenly, I heard him yell, and as I began to rise off my chair, he came flying down the hallway and out the front door! I thought he had hurt himself, so I raced out the door to meet him at his truck, which was parked in the street. He was pale. He told me that "something" had taken hold of his arm. When he turned around he saw a very large man with angry eyes grabbing hold of his upper left arm. It took all the strength he had to free himself from the grip.

The contractor did not know anything about the bedroom or the woman who owned the house before I did. His experience left him shaken. I myself was very concerned about spending any more nights or days in the house, with that "thing" walking about, but I volunteered to go back into the house and return with his tools. I softly prayed to myself as I walked into the bedroom, and I guess God helped me, because I did not see anything.

After he drove away, I walked back to the bedroom and placed a crucifix on the door and closed it. I decided to tell my cousin, who lives in the town just south of Arivaca, about what had happened. "If there is an angry spirit in the bedroom, it must be protecting something. Why wouldn't it want people in the bedroom?" she asked.

That weekend my cousin; her husband, Pablo; and a friend came to my house to investigate. We entered the bedroom and searched the closet and tapped on the walls. As we walked about the room, we all took turns walking over one particular spot on the floor that was colder than the rest of the room. "That's it, it's here!" my cousin said. "What ever this ghost is protecting, it's under this area of the floor."

Pablo went outside and located a small door that was an entrance to a crawl space under the house. He told us to get flashlights. The two men opened the door and entered the crawl space as my cousin and I watched. Soon we heard Pablo yell to us to come outside. The men had found something. As we all gathered in the yard, they showed us a small Indian pottery bowl and some old stone beads. No money, no bones—just a bowl and beads. We placed them into a cardboard box with crumbled up newspaper as packing material.

I didn't want these things in my house, I decided to take

them to the nearby San Javier Del Bac mission at the Pima reservation. After driving up the mission driveway, I waited in my car for a moment, just to think things over. I wasn't sure if giving these Indian things to a priest would be the best thing

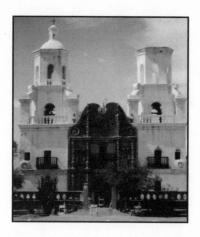

to do. Instead I decided to take a short drive to the reservation office and talk to someone. I met an office worker and explained to her that I needed to know if there was a person who could help me. She gave me directions to the house of a woman who heals people on the reservation.

As I was parking the car on the dirt street, the woman and her son were driving up to the house. I introduced myself and quickly told her about what I had in the cardboard box. She seemed uneasy but said she would take care of it. My meeting with her only took about 15 minutes. I know that I must have appeared very nervous, because I remember speaking to her very quickly. I took the cardboard box with the pot in it from my trunk and left it on her porch. As I drove away, I began to feel very comfortable and relaxed. I somehow knew that I had done the right thing. A feeling of relief came over me.

Since that night I have not had another experience with El Coyote in my house. Today, I use the bedroom as a workshop for ceramic figurines I paint. I paint several different figurines of people, animals, and flowers, but if you look closely you'll notice I don't have one single painted pot. I guess you can tell why I stay away from keeping pots in that bedroom!

BISBEE

The town of Bisbee, is located approximately 100 miles southeast of Tucson, directly in the heart of the Mule Mountains at 5,300 feet above sea level. The quaint town was founded in 1880, and thanks to its rich copper deposits, quickly developed to become the most populated settlement in the state. The city's mineral wealth did not go unnoticed by the Phelps Dodge mining company, who built a railroad into the town in 1880 and soon began to mine the rich ore. The many years of prosperity ended in the early 1970s when Phelps Dodge decided to cease operations, this in turn forced a good number of the town's residents to leave Bisbee and relocate elsewhere.

Today Bisbee is a haven for artists who have settled among the historic buildings and have restored them to their past glory. Bisbee has become a city of diversified yearly events featuring music, crafts and the arts.

The Copper Queen Hotel

The Copper Queen or "The Queen" Hotel was constructed by the Copper Queen Mining Company in the early twentieth cen-

tury. With 45 guest rooms, two
lobbies, Copper Queen Saloon,
patio, swimming pool, and dining room, "The Queen" is Bisbee's major historic landmark.
The hotel is a well-preserved
Victorian style hotel that is
decorated in the manner of the
pioneer West. Given the hotel's
history of hosting such notables
as "Black Jack" Pershing a the
young Teddy Roosevelt, it is no

wonder that a ghost or two (or three) would find such an "invit-
ing" hotel perfect for an extended stay.

The following accounts by the hotel's general manager and
the front desk clerk will provide further evidence for the existence of "other types" of guests at the Copper Queen Hotel.

Craig H. Rothen's Story

I have been the General Manager at the hotel for one year.
Prior to working here, I was living in the Phoenix area and
working as a hotel and restaurant consultant for a corporation
in northern California.

Not long after beginning my position at the hotel, I began to hear stories from several employees about it being haunted. At the time, I regarded all of these stories as nothing more than interesting and funny. I personally have never had any experience with ghosts or hauntings. After about six months into my job, I soon changed my mind when I received a call from two guests who were staying in room 309.

The guests were complaining about the room being very cold. I assured them over the house phone that I would move them into a different room. Once moved, they were pleased with the new room. At approximately 9 a.m., I decided to enter room 309, now empty, to find the cause of the cold temperature. Room 309 operates on its own thermostat, and I thought that perhaps the temperature gauge might be broken.

As I entered the room, I immediately felt a chilling cold envelop my body. I walked

Craig H. Rothen

around the room looking for any open windows. Every window was shut. The air vents were closed, as they should have been. Standing in the middle of the living room, I was at a loss.

Suddenly, the window directly in front of where I was standing opened! I was startled, but not scared. The hotel's windows are not spring loaded so, I was most interested in finding out the cause of the window doing what it did.

I walked up to the open window and did not see any unusual wires or loose springs. Attempting to close the window, I placed both hands on the top window frame and began to apply an even downward pressure. I noticed as I pushed down on the frame, an equal amount of pressure from an unseen force started to push up! I actually felt the power of an invisible force that was resisting my effort to close the window.

Just then, I saw movement next to me on my left. I turned and saw the foggy white image of a presence! I let go of the window and moved my hand right inside this hazy cloud. It felt icy cold to the touch.

Now this is when I knew that something was not normal, I got an eerie feeling that I was not dealing with a normal occurrence. I got the courage to say, "I am going to close the window—*now!*" Once more I placed my hands on the window frame and pushed down. It closed shut easily. I wasted no time in leaving the room.

Just about a month after that incident, late one afternoon, our office had run out of computer paper. I entered the storage closet located on the forth floor to retrieve some paper. As I made my way out of the storage closet, I heard someone call my name, "Craig, Craig." Think-ing I was being called by a co-worker, I answered, "Yes?" There was no answer, and as I looked around, I was alone.

"*I heard someone call my name....*"

I walked down to the third floor where workers were remodeling a room to ask if they called for me. The men answered, "No, we've been busy down here. We haven't taken a break yet." Then they added indifferently, "Mr. Rothen, it must have been the ghost." Not wanting to sound too alarmed by this statement,

I answered, "Yes, thank you," and I walked away.

Just in the year that I've been employed at the hotel, I have had employees come to me with their own stories of ghost encounters in the hotel. One of the housekeepers remarked to me that when she was working during the day shift on the third floor, she saw a little boy who was wrapped in a towel appear to her, only to disappear a few seconds later. Another housekeeper reported to me that on the third floor, the doors open and close on their own.

The curious thing to me is that the hotel has several log books of reported ghostly activities. These written reports give detailed descriptions of the ghostly events including dates, times, etc. These logs books date back over six years. I'll share with you just two short written accounts of what has been recorded. A particular night auditor left the hotel shortly after he wrote the following:

June 8, 1995
I know the ghosts are stirred up again. The phone rang

'Howard' looking very dapper in his hat.

and a gentleman's voice asked for "Howard." I asked Hector, our maintenance man, if he knew who Howard was. Hector had a stunned look on his face. When I listened to the phone once again it was dead. Rose (another employee) who was standing by me said, "It's just Howard checking up on the hotel. Here we go again."

[Howard (deceased) was the name of a front desk clerk who worked for the hotel in the year 1910.]

June 8, 1995

Guest checked out from the third floor. He was awakened by the presence of a ghost. Also, another guest checked out this morning from the third floor. He said he was awakened at 2 a.m. by a beautiful lady, dressed in black, who disappeared.

Laurie Doland's Story

Laurie Doland

I've worked for the Copper Queen now for almost a year as front desk clerk. My first ghost experience took place just three months ago in June at about 2 a.m. I decided to get a drink of water and walked into the dining room, on my way to the kitchen. As I entered the dining room I saw a strange woman standing against one of the columns. She had reddish brown hair which she wore up in a bun, brown eyes, and a healthy pink complexion. She was wearing a high collar blouse and was about in her mid-twenties.

15

Immediately I knew this woman was a ghost I was only able to see her body from the waist up! I stood there, startled. I came upon her so suddenly that the only feeling that came over me was shock. Eventually, my shock turned to fear. We both stood staring at each other for a few seconds, until by chance, the owner of the hotel walked into the dining room. The ghost woman must not have wanted to stay around because she quickly disappeared! I mentioned what I saw to the owner, but she refused to believe what I told her. Since that time, I have not seen the ghost woman again. I have no idea why she chose to appear to me as she did. However, from time to time I have heard both the footsteps, and the movement of a long, crisp, stiff cloth—like a skirt—as it moved across the dining room floor.

Sometimes at night, I'll be visited by another spirit. I'll be alone at the front office, working at the hotel's computer, when I'll suddenly feel the presence of someone walk into the office. I always can tell when this spirit enters the office because the hairs on my arms stand on end, and a thick atmosphere overtakes the room. I'll begin to get a chilling feeling and soon I'm covered in goose bumps. To date, this has happened about five times.

"As I entered the dining room, I saw a strange woman standing against one of the columns."

Fellow male employees have told me about seeing a woman dressed in a black dress who walks up and down the staircase in our lobby. The stairs are located directly in front of the main desk. Interestingly enough, the woman in black chooses to make her appearances only to men. The latest incident with

16

her took place this year, in July, at about 3 a.m. The employee saw the ghost walk down the stairs and enter the dining room. As she walked up to the dining room doors she disappeared!

"The employee saw the ghost walk down the stairs...."

The employee told me that the ghost was dressed in an early 1900s style of dress.

A female employee told me that late one evening when she walked through the dining room, she felt someone grab her shoulder. When she turned around, there was no one there. That was the last time she has ever entered the dining room, day or night!

The sound of a man's heavy shoes walking down the hallways is a very common sound that both guests and employees continually hear in the hotel. I myself have heard these sounds on several occasions. Some nights, in the hotel lobby, I have heard the sounds of unseen people engaged in an uproar of conversation. I can't tell what they are all saying, but they sure do make a ruckus!

Employees always hear their names called out, and when they turn to answer the person they think is calling them, of course there is no one. This happens so frequently that we all now take it in stride. The ghosts are keeping an eye on us.

Another frequent ghost that employees have witnessed is a young boy who runs up and down the halls of the third floor. We also recently had two guests inform the front desk of a woman ghost who they saw dressed in a stripper's costume. The guests reported that this strangely-dressed woman walked down

17

the hall and opened the doors to the third floor veranda. As the guests followed her, she apparently enjoyed the audience, because she started to do a strip tease dance. The dancing ghost did not last for long. In just a few seconds, she disappeared!

Guests in room 312 have reported to us strange bell sounds that wake them from their sleep. Once, two women who were staying in room 312 reported that a hat "appeared" to them, and floated across the room and disappeared.

In Room 212, guests have reported "strong winds" that rattled the doors and windows and kept them up all night. Once these winds rattled a window to the point that it shattered!

I am convinced that the hotel has ghosts, and I'm not the only one who will admit this. Many employees, both past and present, will say the same. The employees are not shy about describing what they have heard and seen.

I haven't heard of any ghosts in the hotel hurting anyone. I think that when these people were alive many years ago they truly enjoyed the Copper Queen, and they still find

"The sound of a man's heavy shoes walking down the hallways is very common...."

it difficult to part with. As far as I can tell, even death has not stopped them from their strong attachment to the hotel.

The Bisbee Inn

In 1916, owner Mrs. S. P. Bedford constructed a 24-room hotel building which today is named The Bisbee Inn. The hotel was furnished by Mrs. Bedford and then leased to Mrs. Kate La More who renamed it the Hotel La More. Rooms at the hotel were $2 per day or $8 per week. For its time, the hotel was advertised as being "the most modern in Bisbee." Between 1922 and 1923, Mrs. La More's hotel lease reverted back to Mrs. Bedford. Mrs. Bedford operated the hotel under the same name (Hotel La More) until she sold it to Grace V. Waters. Various individuals have since owned the hotel. In 1982 Joy and John Timbers bought the property and partially restored it. After their ownership, they ran the hotel as The Bisbee Inn Bed and Breakfast. In 1996 the inn was sold to Elissa and Al Strati, who completed the total restoration of the property.

The current inn is a wonderful and romantic bed and breakfast. Comprised of 20 guest rooms, eight with private baths, the hotel today is a certified historic property. The original oak and period furnishings, together with the walls decorated with photos and maps of years gone by, reflect the present inn's early days of Victorian elegance.

Julie M. Croteau's Story

I interviewed Julie on the front porch of the Inn one warm summer afternoon. My question was direct: "Have you ever been told by guests that there are any ghosts in the Inn?" Julie responded, "Sure, of course, and I'll tell them of my own experiences with ghosts in the building."

Julie M. Croteau

I've been working at the Inn as a maid, laundry person, and front desk clerk for just one year. My first experience with the ghost of the Inn took place in January 1996. It was around 5 pm and I was in the back lounge where the television room is located. Between the room where I was seated and the dining room, were french doors, which were at the time closed.

I noticed movement, and when I turned to look in that direction, I saw a tall man. He was wearing a vest and his jeans were tucked into his high boots. I got the feeling that this was a bizarre guy just by the manner of his dress. Thinking it was a homeless person who had come in off the street looking for a handout, I said, "I'll be right there." I walked down the hallway at the opposite side of the Inn, through the lobby, and then into the dining room. When I entered the dining room, he was gone. I could not have missed anyone passing me in the hall. I immediately knew something strange was going on.

When I later mentioned my experience to other employees, they surprised me with their responses: "Oh, yeah, that's the ghost of the miner guy."

"What?" I said, "You mean you know who I'm talking about?"

"Oh, sure, his ghost appears to us every now and then."

Apparently, I was not the only person who had experienced this ghost. After that, I didn't want to think too much of it, but I've always kept the experience in the back of my mind. I guess the ghost liked me because of what took place next.

A few nights after, I was in my home, seated on the floor watching television. Suddenly, between my television and heater, I saw the image of the ghost I had seen in the Inn, only this time, he was the size of a large doll! Standing as he was, he was was only about three feet tall! I sat there in awe staring eye-to-eye with this thing. Again he was wearing the same outfit as before. He didn't say anything, but slowly began to disappear.

There is another ghost that other employees have seen. This ghost is of a Chinese man. I don't know much more about him, the employee who has seen the man mentioned the experience to me. I guess she doesn't wish to bring up the subject any more than is necessary.

Sometimes, I'll walk down a hall of the Inn, and spot the movement of a shadow at the end of the hall. By now, I'm getting familiar with these shadows. I know that the eyes can play tricks on a person, but the incidents happen so many times that I'm convinced there has got to be more to these experiences than just blurred vision.

All the employees, including myself, have heard doors slamming shut or the banging of metal objects from time to time in the Inn when it is empty. There are cold spots in certain areas of the Inn and one in particular on the stairs. I don't know why this happens, or if there is any rational explanation to these things. I know I've heard these noises and have seen the ghostly shadows. I know that others not familiar with such things might consider me to be odd, but I know that what I've seen is of the paranormal.

I can also tell when something unusual will take place because of a particular flowery scent of lilacs that will permeate the air. It's a pleasant lingering perfume I've noticed in the air of certain rooms of the Inn. I'll be dusting or simply just passing a room, and suddenly the scent will overwhelm me.

21

The scent will come and then leave after a few minutes. The two rooms of the Inn where I've experienced the scents are rooms 8 and 12. I have mentioned this to my co-workers, and they respond casually that they have also smelled the scents, and then add "So what's the big deal?"

CHINLE

Chinle, near the geographic center of the Navajo Indian Reservation in northeastern Arizona, is at the entrance to Canyon de Chelly National Monument. Chinle became a center for population growth and trade after 1868 when the United States signed a treaty with the Navajos. The first trading post was established in 1882, the first mission in 1904, and the first government school in 1910.

Today the community, at an altitude of 5,082 feet, has been designated one of the major "growth centers" on the Navajo Reservation by the tribal government. It is an important trade, administrative, and educational center within the Chinle Chapter (a local government unit) and is headquarters for the Chinle Agency, one of five Bureau of Indian Affairs administrative jurisdictions on the reservation.

I interviewed Josie on the Dineh (Navajo) Reservation not far from the town of Chinle, which is located in the northeast

quadrant of the state. Josie is 41 years, a widowed wife, and mother of twin daughters, aged 16. Our interview took place inside their mobile home, which is situated on deep red, rusty color desert land with wispy juniper trees growing in contorted shapes. Overhead is the endless, vastness of turquoise blue sky.

This location with such unique beauty, would be complete if not for the reality of poverty that lingers all around. Native Americans daily endure such "inconveniences" as no modern plumbing, electricity, or heating, and diets lacking in fresh vegetables and fruits, but rich in fats, sugar and white flour, etc. The outcome of such an existence ultimately leads to obesity and other chronic medical conditions , such as diabetes, heart disease, etc.

The interview was conducted in Josie's kitchen. On the table were various small plastic tubes and glass jars containing a rainbow of assorted, tiny, brightly colored glass beads. Josie and her daughters use these beads to make leather hat bands, necklaces, earrings, and bracelets. Once completed, they take these articles to local stores in town and either sell them or exchange them for personal items.

Josie spoke in a calm, even tone when relating her personal expe-

rience with a witch and ghosts. Her daughters were in the adjoining living room and silently listened as their mother told her story.

Josie's Story

My 70 year old grandfather enjoyed living in the traditional manner of us Navajos in a Navajo round house or "hogan" which is right next to our mobile home. He also prefers to speak only our native language. After my grandmother's death, he lived alone in his hogan for 20 years. Both he and grandmother lived together in a previous hogan, but after she died, grandfather burned it, as is our tradition to do when the owner dies. His new hogan was built for grandfather a short time later, and this is where he now lives.

About eight years ago in the month of November, grandfather—who otherwise was in good health—began to suffer from headaches and body aches that eventually caused him to be bedridden. When grandfather's condition worsened, he began to refuse food. After discussing grandfather's situation with my older brother, we both decided that it would be best to take him to a doctor in WindowRock. Grandfather was hesitant but soon realized the logic of our decision to seek medical help. After being admitted into the clinic, he was taken through the long process of many blood tests and x-rays. My brother and I spent three days in Window Rock at a friend's house, while grandfather was being cared for. When the results of the tests eventually came back from the lab, to our surprise and relief, they indicated that he only had a rise in blood sugar, which could be treated with drugs. Aside from this, his other tests were normal.

However, both my brother and I were not totally convinced that all was well with him. We had seen the turn for the worse, that our otherwise active and mentally alert grandfather had taken. His state of constant pain and fatigue was very unusual for him. The doctor prescribed pain medicine to help him sleep. After filling the prescriptions, we returned home.

On the return drive home, grandfather stated that he wanted to seek the help of a local medicine man in Chinle. Grandfather wanted to have a Sing. Among us Navajos, we have a curing ceremony which we call a Sing. The Sing ceremony involves the participation of an elder medicine man or woman. Special songs are sung, incense is burned, and a drum and other ritual items are used. It is a lengthy ceremony and highly respected among traditional Navajos. My brother and I assured my grandfather that we would honor his wishes and contact a medicine man back home.

Arrangements were made with an elderly medicine man, and a date for the Sing was set. Four nights before the ceremony, a strange thing happened to me.

It had been snowing heavily during the day and that evening. The moon was bright and full. At around 11 p.m., I was awakened by the barking of our dog, who we keep chained to our porch. Usually she barks at skunks that live under the mobile home, or in response to the yelping of coyotes that sometimes come around our property. This time her barking sounded different to me. It made me get out of my warm bed and walk to the window. As I parted the curtains on the front door, I saw a woman whom I did not recognize, walking around my grandfather's hogan. I reached for my jacket and boots, and walked outside.

My dog kept growling and barking. In the moonlit night, I watched this strange woman make her way to the rear of the hogan. When I yelled at her, "What do you want?" She did not respond. I decided to confront this strange woman. With my dog still barking loudly, I quickly made my way to the hogan as my footsteps crunched noisily into the foot-deep snow.

When I was about 20 feet away from the woman, I saw that

she was wrapped in a dark shawl from head to toe. Her face was hidden from my sight. Something inside me made me immediately stop in my tracks. As soon as I stopped, the woman suddenly turned away from me. What happened next made my mouth open wide.

The dark woman took off like a flash! She did not run but seemed to float over the snow-covered ground without leaving a trace of footsteps! My dog barked and barked. I turned in the direction of the trailer, and ran back. I missed a step and remember taking a hard fall. Once I reached the trailer I rushed inside and locked the door! Both my daughters told me that they had witnessed the whole affair from the safety of the mobile home window. I was out of breath and shaking. I knew that I had seen something evil outside. My girls were also shaken, and that night we all slept together.

The next day I wasted no time in telling my experience to my brother. After hearing my story, he knew that what had taken place that night had to be witchcraft. A ghost or witch had for some reason visited our home. My brother said, "Who knows how long these evil visits have been going on without us being aware of them?" We all decided that it would be best not to tell our grandfather for fear that such information would upset him. We didn't want to risk him becoming even more ill.

We also knew that this new information needed to be related to the medicine man. My brother drove me to the medicine man's home, and we informed him of what I had seen. He was not surprised by my story. He said, "Oh, I know who this is." Then he explained to us that there was a Navajo medicine woman who lived not far from his house who wanted to gain the reputation in the Indian community as being a powerful spiritual person.

After I heard the medicine man's description of this woman, I could recall her from a visit she made to my grandfather's hogan several weeks before grandfather became ill. I remember grandfather telling me that this woman had visited him because she wanted him to be her boyfriend. When grandfather refused, she got very angry at him and yelled obscenities. She left our property in a rage!

The medicine man further explained, "It is difficult to gain power without earning it in the correct manner. This woman has decided to seek the help of certain animal spirits instead of asking the Creator for direction, and doing what is right." He also said, "You need to know that this woman wants to hurt your grandfather. Your grandfather refused to do what she demanded, so now she has taken revenge. She chose to make him ill, but she will not stop until he is dead." My brother and I could not understand why this medicine woman would want to be so evil as to hurt our grandfather. Our concern now was for our grandfather to be healed. The medicine man said that he would be ready to confront this woman's witchcraft during grandfather's Sing.

The night of the ceremony came and we all gathered inside my grandfather's hogan. We used kerosene lamps for light, and a fire was started in the wood stove. Soon the medicine man arrived and the ceremony began. Grandfather was seated on a blanket placed on the dirt floor. In front of him, the medicine man placed the items that would be used for the "cleansing": a bowl of water, a leather bag of corn pollen, a basket that held a beautiful eagle feather, and various other items. The medicine man began to drum and sing his songs, calling the positive forces of Mother Earth and the four directions. He sang towards the heavens and asked the Creator for vision, help, and power in defeating all evil. His singing continued for about an hour or so. He reached for the basket which held the eagle feather and grabbed hold of the feather's stem. Saying a prayer, he passed the feather over grandfather's head and body. Then, the medicine man returned the feather to the basket and closed his eyes.

All our eyes were focused on the medicine man's face as it began to slowly. His eyes closed tightly, and his mouth began to display a severe expression of pain. His clenched teeth were very noticeable in the warm orange glow of the lanterns. I held on to my brother's arm so strongly that know I must have left bruise marks. I was scared from watching what was taking place before us. This small elderly old man seated on the ground before us was changing into something "spiritual." A force had taken over him and what we were seeing was scaring me. Grandfather was so weak with illness that I had to brace his body with one hand so he wouldn't fall over. As grandfather closed his eyes and prayed silently, he was unaware of the transformation that was taking place in the medicine man.

With a quick motion, the medicine man suddenly turned over on all fours, and with the gestures of a determined dog or wolf, began to crawl around, sniffing the air and pawing at the ground! He then crawled his way to a corner of the hogan and began to dig vigorously with his bare hands at the dirt floor. His breathing became loud and filled with energy. He dug and dug with the force of a man much younger and stronger than he.

I took a quick glance at my brother. His face showed that he was also in awe at what was taking place. I returned my eyes to the medicine man who had now dug a hole about a foot deep. Then he stopped his digging and seemed to recover from his "trance." In a dazed voice, the medicine man asked my brother to bring a lamp over to him, which he quickly did. Then, the medicine man reached into the hole he had just dug, and to all our amazement, pulled out a soil-covered sweater that belonged to my grandfather!

The medicine man stated, "Here is what the witch used for her evil medicine against your grandfather, but now I will use it against her. She used this sweater as her only way to witch him. She will no longer be able to have control over him!" After saying this, he sang a song while placing the eagle feather

29

and corn pollen over the head and shoulders of my grandfather. My grandfather took a deep breath and fell to one side. My brother was ready to catch him as he fell. Grandfather must have gone through a lot of effort, because he said that he was tired and wanted to sleep. We left him there in his hogan covered in warm wool blankets. The ceremony was over.

We followed the medicine man outside the hogan as he carried the sweater and placed it on the ground. He asked for a lamp, and then emptied the kerosene from a lamp over the sweater. He lit a match and tossed it upon the sweater. The fire slowly began to burn and consumed it. Suddenly, in the distance, we heard a piercing loud scream or howl. We turned in the direction of the sound and I spotted a ball of light appeared that rose up high into the sky, then it bounced away into the desert! The medicine man informed us that what we had just heard and seen was the witch. "She will never be able to recover her strength, I found her power, and she will be eaten up by her own evil."

After that night, grandfather returned to his old self. I am convinced of the powers that some bad people can use to harm others. So much jealously and evil exists in the world. However, it is good to know that in the end, the power of the Creator always wins. I have seen it.

CHINO VALLEY

Chino Valley is the site of the first territorial capital of Arizona. The capital moved to Prescott, 15 miles away, in 1864. U.S. Army Cavalry Lt. Amiel W. Whipple, while traveling through the area in 1854, gave the community its name. "Chino" is the Mexican name for the abundant curly grama grass growing in the area.

In 1895, a narrow-gauge branch of the United Verde and Pacific Railroad to Jerome joining the Prescott and Arizona Central was completed, and Jerome Junction was established. Between 1900 and 1925, the activities of Jerome Junction were absorbed by Chino Valley.

The town is in north central Arizona, on state Highway 89, 15 miles north of Prescott and 35 miles south of Ash Fork, which is on Interstate 40. It was incorporated in 1970 and is at an elevation of 4,750 feet.

The economy of Chino Valley is based on a mix of retail, commercial and government activities. With the significant growth in Chino Valley, employment has been created in construction, service and supplies. Agriculture is also a viable business.

Lisa and Geri's Story

My interview with Lisa and her partner of 33 years, Geri, took place in their home, twenty miles south of Chino Valley in the nearby town of Prescott. The women purchased the house and 15 acres in Chino Valley in 1962 from a woman who had lived in the house for only three months. Lisa and Geri were attending a party in Phoenix, and by chance, happened to meet the seller of the property. As their conversation progressed, the seller informed Lisa and Geri about the home. That night Lisa and Geri made arrangements to meet her at the property the next day. They drove 150 miles north to Chino Valley and immediately fell in love with the old two-story house and surrounding land.

What now follows is both women's story of an incredible ghostly experience. I don't believe many people would chose to remain in such a negative house unless they had to. What happened to Lisa and Geri in their home is a testament to their strong will to conquer what evil existed in the house. Did they eventually overcome this evil presence?

Lisa's Explanation

After buying the property, Geri and I immediately went to work. With a hammer in each hand and the will to make a home out of a real "fixer-upper" we set our goal to start with the most important rooms: the kitchen and bath. The bedrooms were next, followed by the living room and dining room. We decided to leave the outside of the house for last. The roof had been patched six years before with hot tar, so we felt it could withstand the elements for another year or two.

We spent the days in our new house, hard at work. Our evenings were spent in a beat-up old trailer we had bought and parked on the property. It was nice to have the trailer to relax in after a day of dust and sweat. Eventually, the kitchen was completed and in a few days, so was the bathroom. The two upstairs bedrooms were next. Strange things began to happen to both of us after we decided one day to tackle the bedrooms.

One morning after having breakfast, I left Geri at the kitchen table reading the paper as I walked up the short flight of stairs to the second floor. As I reached the top floor, the door in one of the bedrooms slammed shut with a loud bang. The noise was loud enough to startle one of our small dogs. He ran right up the stairs and up to the door where he excitedly barked and barked.

Geri, who was in the kitchen, called out to me, "Hey, what's going on up there?"

I answered, "Nothing, the wind just blew the door shut."

Geri called to our dog, who was still upstairs with me, and as he ran down the stairs, I approached the door and reached for the knob. I turned the knob and pushed on the door to open it. I heard the clicking sound that the knob made, but it would not open. I thought it might have gotten stuck from the force of the slam, so I played with it for a second or two. I managed to open it about an inch, then it came flying right back to its closed position. I had the feeling that something was not right. I called to Geri, "Get up here right now!" I told her that I thought someone was in the bedroom. We readied ourselves for the possibility of encountering a prowler. Again, I turned the knob and pushed on the door. This time it gave a little and with Geri's help, it opened.

We entered the bedroom and immediately felt a cold chill. An overwhelming feeling of what I can only describe as a heaviness or thickness hung in the atmosphere of the room. Geri said, "Let's get the hell out of here!" We both rushed down the stairs and into the kitchen. Noticing our excitement, our two little dogs barked like crazy animals. Needless to say, we decided to leave the cleaning of the bedrooms for another day. The memory of what had happened to us that morning stayed with us throughout the day.

That evening we were having our dinner, once again sitting at the kitchen table. Our only form of entertainment at the time was the radio, which was plugged into one of the few working electrical outlets in the house, in the living room. Suddenly, our dogs began to bark. Above our heads on the second floor, Geri and I heard the hurried footsteps of someone suddenly running from one end of the bedroom to the other. We looked at each other and froze still! Between the footsteps, the barking dogs and the music on the radio, our senses became overloaded. We were scared and again concerned that someone might be in the house. Geri stayed in the kitchen while I ran to the trailer. Ready to confront any burglar, I loaded our shotgun and returned to the kitchen.

With the dogs leading the way, Geri and I cautiously walked up the stairs. Geri reached for the light switch, and the single light bulb hanging from wires at the top of the stairs turned on. Our dogs dashed into the same bedroom where we had experienced the negative vibes earlier in the day, then they ran out crying as if someone had hit them. I immediately thought, no S.O.B. was going to hit our dogs. I yelled out, "Hey, we've got a gun, get out of the room now!" The only sound we heard was the sound of our dogs barking behind us. Then I yelled out, "I said, I've got a gun; get out now!" There was no answer. We decided to enter the room anyway.

We soon discovered that there was no one in the bedroom. We checked the closet and opened the closed window and looked outside. No one. We then checked the adjacent bedroom, and again the window was closed shut and it was empty. We were at a loss to explain what was going on.

We sat down at the top of the stairs trying to make sense of something which made no sense. Geri began to cry, and I placed my arm around her. She was really frightened. Just then we heard a hideous laugh, followed once again by the slamming sound of the bedroom door! I got up and pointed the gun to the door, "Get out here I say. Out here now!" The laughter began again and with a courage that even surprised me, I walked to the door and turned the knob and kicked it open. The room was empty! That was enough for us. We took off out of the house and spent the most nervous night we ever had locked in our trailer.

In the comforting light of the morning, we walked out of the trailer and whistled for our dogs. The dogs were nowhere to be seen. They were probably out among the desert brush chasing a skunk or something. I grabbed my gun once again, and we cautiously re-entered the house. It was strange to be walking softly, as though we were visitors in our own house, but we did not want to take any chances. Up stairs nothing seemed strange or out of place. The feeling was a totally different from the frightful night before; everything seemed calm and peaceful.

As the morning progressed into the afternoon, we began to return back to our normal working routine. When one of our dogs reappeared, Geri became concerned about the whereabouts of our other dog.

After searching for a few minutes, Geri came running to where I was mixing paint. Geri cried, "Come look. I found our other dog, and she's dead!" I followed her inside the house to the living room. There in the corner, where a water pipe was exposed next to the wall was our little dog. Her head was strangely lodged tightly between the wall and the pipe! There was no rational reason for this to have taken place. None at all.

We had to forcefully pull the pipe away from the wall in order to dislodge our poor dog's head. We buried her in the yard and of course, cried for days. Everything was so mysterious to us-the footsteps, the laughter, the slamming doors, the eerie feelings in the bedroom, and now the death of our dog.

The weeks passed, and we did not experience any further strange happenings. The energy and time that we had put into the house was showing. It looked great! We then progressed to the second floor. We started with the farthest bedroom. After that one was completed, we entered the bedroom where we had weeks before experienced the ghostly happenings.

The walls were covered in a very old print wallpaper, which we wanted to immediately remove. There were faded square marks on the wallpaper that showed where picture frames had hung for many years. Geri was going to tackle the removal of the paper, while I scraped the old paint off the window and door. Geri can next tell you what she discovered.

Geri's Explanation

As I was tearing away the old wallpaper, I reached a part of the wall about two feet above the floor. I pulled the paper away from this section of the wall and underneath were what appeared to be bloodstains on the wallboard! I called Lisa to look at this and to give me her opinion. She also said that it appeared to be old, dried blood. We got goose bumps. I quickly tore away the rest of the paper. And as soon as Lisa finished mixing the paint, I painted over the wall and the stains. The following day we brought in a bed, dresser, small table, and a lamp. We were done at last!

We had a gathering of friends one day who had traveled from Phoenix who greeted us with house warming gifts. They loved the house and the decorating we spent so much effort on. Five of our visitors chose not to make the long return drive home that evening, so they decided to spend the night. We stayed up late that night eating, drinking, and enjoying each other's company, in the living room.

Suddenly, we heard a loud crash come from the upstairs bedroom. We ran up the stairs, and when I tried to open the door, I found that it was not opening. Now, with all our friends witnessing, I pushed and pushed. Just as before, I knew that there was someone inside the bedroom pushing against my efforts. I could feel the power of the "person" playing tug of war with me. A friend came to my rescue, and with her help we opened the door wide.

We were not ready for the scene of destruction that the bedroom was in. The lamp lay broken on the floor, and blankets were all about the room. Strangest of all was the wall by the bed. The blood stains had reappeared! They had come through the newly painted wall!

We all were taken aback by the sight. Our friend said, "Girls, you've got ghosts in this house!" Lisa and I kept quiet, and we knew she was right. With the help of our friends, we cleaned the mess in the bedroom and returned to the living room. Lisa and I informed our friends of the other happenings we had experienced months before. Everyone was shocked to hear our story and as the discussion progressed. Suddenly from the upstairs came that horrible laugh once again. We all heard it!

Our friend Yolanda let out a scream! We pleaded with everyone to help us solve this thing once and for all. We decided to walk up the stairs and talk to the ghost and ask it to leave the house. There was strength in numbers, so up we went to the bedroom. The bedroom door was wide open. On the bed we had just remade, lay clothes. The pieces of clothes were arranged on the

bed in the form of a body! The only thing missing was the actual body. They were neatly placed in such a way as to give us the impression that a body was lying in a coffin! The arms of the shirt were folded at the elbows and crossed over the chest.

I grabbed the clothes and threw them back into the closet. We decided to immediately hold hands and form a circle and pray. We prayed to Jesus to remove this ghost, or ghosts, and to forever cleanse our house of any evil. We took turns asking for blessings and help. Suddenly in the middle of our "ceremony" we heard the quick footsteps of someone rushing down the stairs and out the kitchen door! We held on to each other's hands with such force. I cried and thanked Jesus for getting rid of the ghost. I knew that would be the end of our hauntings. We all felt so wonderful after that. Thankfully, we have not had any more ghostly things happen to us since that night.

DOUGLAS

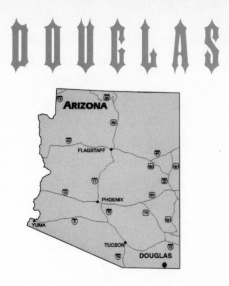

Douglas, on the Mexican border, is 118 miles southeast of Tucson, and is reachable via Interstate 10 to U.S. 80. Across the border from Douglas is Agua Prieta in Sonora, Mexico. The Janos Highway, the shortest route to Mexico City and Guadalajara by paved roads from the western United States, begins in Douglas.

Douglas, at an elevation of 3,990 feet, was founded in 1901 as a site for a copper smelter and was incorporated in 1905. Originally, it was an annual round-up spot for ranchers. Agriculture and ranching are still important segments of the area's economy.

Nandy and Victoria Ryan

Our interview took place in the Ryan's wonderfully-restored, hundred year old adobe house, which they purchased over 40 years ago. Victoria and her husband, Nandy, currently occupy the house. They have a son who was raised in the house, but he did not personally experience any ghostly events. Their son currently lives in California and teaches at a state university.

The Ryans, now retired, have furnished their house throughout the years with very old pieces of furniture and folk art from old Mexico.

Very early on in their marriage, the "travel bug bit them." Subsequently, through their travels, they've come to know and make many friends.

The house has the appearance of a folk museum, with a wonderful display of very old hand-made wooden furniture and many other works of Mexican folk art- masks, dolls, weavings, etc.

The massive wooden vigas or beams that support the ceiling of the house were also brought over from Mexico when the Ryans remodeled their house. The vigas were taken from a church built in the late 1700s in the Mexican state of Chihuahua. The church was abandoned on land that Mexican friends of the Ryans had purchased. Knowing the Ryans might want the hand-carved vigas for their home, the friends in Mexico had the 50 or so vigas trucked to Doughlas as a gift to the Ryans. The old vigas can now be viewed in all their antique splendor as they decorate the ceiling overhead.

Aside from the already mentioned vigas and decorations, the whole house has most of the original plank flooring, including the many scratches, knots, and imperfections that add so much to the character of the house. I couldn't help but mention the loud snapping, and creaking sounds the floor made when I walked over it. Victoria responded, "Yes, it takes a little getting used to, doesn't it?" Aside from the annoying floor noises, Victoria and Nandy have experienced quite a lot of other "disturbances" in their home.

I arrived at their house at 4 p.m. and I finished the interview at 10 p.m. Aside from their story of the paranormal, they had many other stories regarding their travels thatkept me wide-eyed and hanging on each word they spoke, stories that were incredibly interesting, filled with their adventures.

The Ryan's Story

As you can see, the house has a lot of special things that we enjoy collecting. It can make some visitors feel overwhelmed.

We use that old red *trastero* (dish cabinet) over there against the living room wall to display Victoria's doll collection. It has an interesting story in itself.

When we first noticed weird occurrences taking place in the house, we knew it had to be a ghost. My wife's art supplies began to do some strange things. This might sound crazy, but her brushes moved on their own. We both watched as the brushes lifted themselves out of the metal can and fell on the table or floor! The brushes rolled a few feet and then came to a stop. We knew that this had to be the work of a ghost. What else could it be? This happened only twice, and Victoria joked that if she could train the ghost to paint on canvas, we would be rich indeed.

The next experience we had took place one November morning, about two months later, in the early morning hours of the night. We both were awakened from our sound sleep by the noise of the floor boards in the living room creaking, as if someone were walking about the house. Thinking it might be a burglar after our collections, I got out of bed and carefully walked to the living room, only to discover that there was not a soul in the house—so to speak.

Victoria also got out of bed, and we inspected every drawer, showcase, and cabinet for missing itemS. Everything was in its place, except for her paint brushes, which were tossed about the living room floor! We immediately thought that a possum or other animal might have entered the house and caused all the noise and mess. Our theory soon changed when we started to hear soft laughter in a kind of whispering voice. We both were able to hear this voice and it frightened us. After a few seconds, the laughter slowly went away. "Well," I said to Victoria, "our ghost is back!"

Just three days later, at about 4 p.m., I was in the kitchen making a sandwich when I heard someone say, "Nandy, you stupid man, you are a stupid man, why are you so stupid?" I turned around expecting to see someone, but I was alone, and

Victoria was in the front yard watering her apricot tree. I walked out to ask Victoria if she called me stupid. When I saw her sitting beside the tree pulling out the weeds, well, I knew she would not be so cruel as to call me such names. I told her about what I had heard in the kitchen. With a surprised expression on her face, she told me that the same thing had happened to her earlier that same morning! Not wanting to worry me, she had decided it would be best to not mention it to me.

We had a strong suspicion that things were not going to go very well from then on, Especially when the ghost was now speaking to us unkindly. We decided to give the ghost no further attention, hoping that perhaps by ignoring it, it would find some other house to haunt.

That same night, we heard a whispering voice that seemed to be coming from the ceiling above our heads. Try as we could, we were unable to make sense out what the whispering voice was saying. This last episode made us feel annoyed and a little bit scared.

The sound of someone walking about the house was now becoming a regular day and night experience for us. Then things really took off. We began to predict when the ghost would want to start trouble, because we would begin to feel a chilling cold temperature change in the house, Even in the month of June when the weather is already quite hot. Once the noises began, the living room always stayed the coldest room in our house. The doors on the old red *trastero* would also quickly opened on their own and loudly be slammed shut by an unseen hand. It was terrible.

The ghost next chose my wife's doll collection to vent its anger. Apparently, the ghost did not like the dolls because we found them tossed about the living room. One morning we discovered one doll in the toilet, head first.

Another very scary experience with the ghost, was when our religious items began to be attacked. In our collection, we have several religious statues from old Mexico, New Mexico, and

Guatemala. The statues are placed throughout the house, and we would find them turned to face the wall! We have a small crucifix that I had placed above our bed, which also was turned to face the wall. Once we saw this side of the ghost's anger, well, we said enough is enough and decided to call a local priest for help.

It so happened that the Catholic priest was out of town for a week, so we instead contacted an Episcopalian priest who agreed to bless our house. We were surprised when the priest informed us that given his busy schedule, he would conduct the house blessing the following morning. This was good news for us, but when we returned home our ghost must have known something was about to change, because of what happened next.

As soon as we returned home from our visit with the priest and turned on the lights, I saw a dark figure quickly dash from the living room to the kitchen! Victoria and I had never seen such a thing in the house. Just about an hour later, as we were both seated in the living room watching television, a small clay vase on a side table fell to the floor. Luckily, due to the thick carpet it didn't break. I picked up the vase and placed it in a box inside a closet. This was enough.

We felt that it would be a good idea to light a few white candles and place them in each room of the house. After doing this, we again sat in the living room and watched television until we felt sleepy. We snuffed out all the candles in the house except for the one in our bedroom. We didn't want to risk having the ghost get so angry that it would want to start a fire.

Throughout the night, we kept hearing footsteps pacing across the the floors of the house. The ghost was apparently upset and was making sure we were well aware of its distress. At one point, we heard a loud "thud" followed by the sound of rocks being dropped on the floor. I got out of bed and walked to each room and saw nothing out of place. I then stated, "Knock it off, you'll soon be gone from this house, so be still!" After that, I went to bed, and we didn't hear anymore noise.

At 9 a.m. the following morning, there was a knock on the front door. It was the priest. He entered, and I offered him some coffee. Being in a bit of a hurry, he declined my offer and got to the business of ridding the house of our unwelcome ghost.

The ritual of a house blessing did not take longer than a half hour or so. During the ritual nothing unusual happened, except that we kept smelling a strong odor of what I can only describe as iron or sulfur. That was about it. The priest left our home and all appeared to be well.

Victoria and I decided that it would be a good idea to thoroughly clean the house, so we gathered together a mop, broom and dust pan and got to work. As we carefully moved furniture and rugs, it came time to move the red *trastero*. When I looked underneath the *trastero*, I noticed the floor had a thick layer of wall plaster that must have come loose from the adobe wall. As we each took hold of one end to slide the *trastero* away from the living room wall, an even larger portion of plaster fell from the wall directly behind it. The thought then hit me: " so this must have been the noise I had heard the night before of dirt or rocks hitting the wooden floor."

In the light of day, we could see that the fallen plaster had been covering a small wooden door frame that had been built into the living room wall many years before. We were at a loss to guess why someone would have built such a thing and place it in a wall, and then wall it up with plaster?

We both concluded that the ghostly noises must have been due to whatever this little door represented. I located a small picture of the Virgin of Guadalupe and a small metal crucifix and pinned them to the small door. I then mixed some new plaster and replastered the wall, sealing the religious articles within the wall.

Since that time we have had no further disturbances. Why the ghost was upset, we have no clue. Why it waited all these years to show its anger is still a mystery to us. We are sure glad to have it gone and hope it stays gone!

FLAGSTAFF

Flagstaff, located at the intersection of Interstate 17 and I-40, is the largest city and regional center of northern Arizona. It is county seat for Coconino, the second largest U.S. county with 12 million acres. Flagstaff, at 7,000 feet, is one of the highest U.S. cities and its breath-taking backdrop is even higher. The community sits at the base of San Francisco Peaks, Arizona's highest point at 12,633 feet.

Flagstaff is a year-round mecca for visitors. Many Arizonans maintain second homes here. Summer temperatures average 20 degrees cooler than Phoenix (146 miles south on Interstate 17). In the winter there is skiing, ice skating and hunting.

Flagstaff has long been a transportation hub. Located along an old wagon road to California, Flagstaff was established after the railroad arrived in 1881. Today the town links I-40 to I-17, Highway 89 to Page and Utah, and Highway 180 to the Grand Canyon. Historic Route 66 passes through Flagstaff.

Flagstaff's name comes from a tall pine tree that was made into a flagpole in 1876 to celebrate the Declaration of Independence Centennial.

Flagstaff is a governmental, educational, transportation, cultural, and commercial center. Tourism is a major source of employment. Traditional economic activities continue to employ people.

Marcus and Ginger LaPorte

I interviewed husband and wife, Marcus and Ginger, at their home one evening. The LaPortes are a couple in their late 40S who have lived in Flagstaff since 1977. They met and married in the Louisiana city of New Orleans. *They now live in a large two-story log home, six miles north of Flagstaff's central district. We sat down for a long comfortable conversation in their living room. The living room has three very large floor-to-ceiling picture windows, which allowed me to view the beautiful night sky throughout my visit. As their story developed, I soon began to feel a little bit nervous. Needless to say, it was a scary one.*

Their story will make the reader pause, and think twice about ever again, purchasing "bargain items" at yard sales. What follows is a story that can happen in any state to anyone. The LaPortes simply were a couple who happened to be unaware of anything related to ghosts in their personal lives. As you will now read,such an attitude does not necessarily prevent ghosts from reaching out to touch the living.

The LaPorte's Story

Marcus and I decided one July weekend to clean out our garage and basement. It is incredible how much "junk" we had stored away throughout the years. We decided that the best thing to do with all the used clothes and odds and ends was to hold a yard sale. We placed an advertisement in the local paper and got to work cleaning out the house. We informed some of our neighbors about the upcoming sale, and word quickly spread around. Marcus also spoke to his mother, who moved to Flagstaff two years ago. He convinced her that the yard sale

would be a great way to sell some of the antiques she brought from her home town of New Orleans. Although at first she was reluctant to even think of parting from her cherished antiques, she thought about it for a moment and then changed her mind.

The date was set and when the Saturday sale took place we found more "junk" and treasures than we had realized we ever owned. Marcus' mother's antiques were a big hit. A neighbor of Chinese decent, came by before the 8 a.m. starting time and bought a dresser of mother's. This dresser was not a very pretty piece of furniture at all. It needed some refinishing and the mirror was particularly in need of restoring. However, our neighbor said she "loved it" and she had a space in her guest room where it would look great!

I could tell that Mother LaPorte was very eager to part with this piece of furniture. I asked her why she was so eager to sell the dresser, when just a few days ago she would not even want to consider selling any of her antiques. She answered, "Well, I should have gotten rid of that evil thing a long time ago." Her words made me ask what she meant by referring to a piece of furniture as "evil." She responded, "Oh, it's nothing dear, just nothing." I could tell by her voice that she wanted to drop the subject, so I didn't ask her any further questions.

Over all, the sale was a big success, and most of mother's antiques did sell. What remained of the unsold clothes and junk we donated to a local charity. That was the end of that—so we thought.

About a month later, our neighbor who bought the dressER phoned me and described a very strange thing that had happened to their family. She said that she had removed the dresser from the guest room, and it was now in their garage with a carpet draped over it. She started to describe the trouble she and her family had experienced. I was so interested in the little she did say that I asked her to hold her thoughts and come right over to our house. I wanted her to tell her story in the presence of Marcus and his mother. I informed mother of some of the story which our neighbor told to me over the phone. Mother responded by saying, "Let's just wait to hear what she has to say." Soon there was a knock on the door and I showed the neighbor in. We sat around the kitchen table and she told the most incredible and scary story I have ever heard.

Our neighbor started her story by saying that after purchasing the antique dresser from our yard sale, she dusted it off and placed the dresser in her guest room. "I loved it," she said "I even bought a blue flower vase and a brass brush and comb set that I knew would enhance its look. These I placed on top of a white doily on the dresser. It looked beautiful. I also went out and purchased a cute little embroidered boudoir stool and placed it in front of the dresser. It was now complete."

The following weekend, her daughter came to visit from Phoenix and spent the night in the guest room. During the night, the daughter said that she was awakened by a noise in the room. She slowly opened her eyes and saw that seated at the dresser, was a strange blonde-haired woman. The woman was busy brushing her hair. she then noticed that the neighbor's daughter was watching her and turned to face her. In a split second, the blonde woman was standing at the side of her bed!

Her daughter was shocked to see this stranger in her room. She watched as this ghostly woman violently waved her arms above her head. The daughter noticed that the ghost woman was opening her mouth wide and making facial gestures which gave the impression that the ghost was screaming with hatred or pain but, strangely, made no sounds.

Soon the daughter found the courage to grab her pillow, which she threw at the ghost. Immediately, the image of the ghost woman disappeared. With tear filled eyes, the daughter turned on the lights and sat on the side of the bed trying to compose herself. She was not sure what had taken place. Did she dream it, or was she visited by an actual ghost? She soon grew tired and leaving the bedroom light on, crawled under the covers and fell back to sleep.

In the morning, the daughter told her mother about what she experienced the night before, describing it as a nightmare. Our neighbor told us that she was fascinated by her daughter's story but skeptical. However, our neighbor's skepticism soon ended when they both went up to the dresser and discovered that on the new brush and comb set were several strands of blond hair! Since they are Chinese, our neighbor, her husband, and daughter all have quite dark hair. Whose hair was on the brush?

Our neighbor lifted up the brush with the blonde hair strands and showed her daughter. The daughter, very apprehensively stated, "Well, see, now you have the evidence in your hand. I told you there was a woman in this room with me." Our neighbor needed no further explanations. Immediately she and her daughter removed the dresser from the guest bedroom and placed it in the garage where it was covered with an old carpet. The brush with the blond hair was wrapped within paper towels, placed in a plastic bag, and disposed of in the trash.

Since that night they had not been visited by the ghost, but the neighbor wanted to know if Mother LePorte wanted to buy back her antique dresser. Marcus' mother said she would, and arrangements were made to place the dresser back in storage. Not once did Mother LePorte add anything to the neighbor's story. In fact, mother just sat quietly in her chair listening to the conversation.

After the neighbor left our house that evening, Marcus' mother surprised us by telling us that she had a similar visit from the strange blond woman, when the dresser was in her own bedroom, several years ago in New Orleans. She had purchased the dresser from an elderly African-American gentleman. He explained to her that the dresser, among other furniture he was selling at the time, was from an estate sale. Apparently, the furniture and the few other items he was selling were all that remained of a disastrous house fire. Several family members were burned to death in that fire.

Marcus' mother had her own ghostly experience with the dresser one the evening. One night she heard a voice coming from her bedroom. As she walked into the bedroom to investigate, she was surprised to see a strange woman standing by the dresser. The blonde haired woman stood with her hands raised and clutched together in front of her. She was dressed in a light blue nightgown and had an expression of dread on her face. Marcus' mother asked the woman, "Who are you? How did you get here?" Incredibly, the woman's image immediately disappeared. Marcus' mother had never experienced anything like this before. It was only after she brought the dresser into the bedroom that the ghost appeared. The

"The dresser now sits in a storage unit."

dresser must be spiritually associated somehow with its original owner. "I know it's the dresser," she said "I could feel it in my soul that that dresser had something to do with the ghost."

Mother LaPorte wasted no time in removing the dresser from the bedroom to the porch at the rear of the house, where it stood for several years. The ghost of the blonde woman was not seen again until this most recent time in Flagstaff.

The dresser now sits in a Flagstaff storage unit. Who knows where it will eventually end up? For now, the ghost will have to just wait before she can reappear to someone else. Maybe then she'll tell her story instead of just scaring people.

FLORENCE

Florence is in Pinal County midway between Phoenix and Tucson. Colonel Levi Ruggles, an Indian agent, staked and plotted the town in 1866. Sources cite different origins for the town's name, but all agree it was someone's sister or daughter. By the 1920s, the area had become the agricultural center of the county.

The Florence business district is still on Main Street, and aside from the obvious improvements, downtown looks much as it must have in the 1880s. Both visitors and residents appreciate the diversity of the community. Florence offers the convenience and lifestyle available in a small western community, yet is only 45 minutes away from the Phoenix and Tucson metropolitan areas. Incorporated in 1908, Florence, at an elevation of 1,493 feet, has been the county seat since its formation in 1875.

Nancy L. Corrales' Story

I interviewed Nancy at her home located on the far east portion of the city. Nancy is a 50 year old divorced woman with two teenage boys. *Nancy's family is originally from the state of Texas; her parents moved to Florence in the 1930s to work as farm workers in the cotton fields. Her story is about a peculiar uncle named Edward, or as she referred to him, Uncle Eddie." Uncle Eddie was Nancy's mother's older brother who lived with the Corrales family until his death in 1954.*

After divorcing her husband in 1979, Nancy returned to Florence, to the home where she spent her youth. The house is an old one-story adobe brick house, with a large rusted sheet metal roof. These days Nancy spends her days tending to her rose and vegetable gardens, and some evenings she can be found at the local church bingo. "I live a peaceful life here in Florence. I love my neighbors very much. Everyone is so kind to each other," she said.

Nancy also stated, "My uncle was a really 'special' man. Once you hear my story about him, you'll know why." What follows is my interview with Nancy and her experience with the ghost of Uncle Eddie.

Growing up in a small town like Florence was really fortunate for a young girl like me. I enjoyed the freedom and safety of being able to go to the grocery store and not worry about being assaulted. Even though I carried no money, all I was required to do was to sign my name on a receipt and at the end of each month, my parents would total up the charges and pay their bill. What bothered me was not being allowed to buy candy—just milk, eggs, and bread.

Sometimes, after returning from work, my Uncle Eddie would accompany me to the store. His favorite thing was to treat me to a candy bar. He would also buy two bottles of beer, which he would take to his friend's house. Uncle Eddie and his friend would both drink their beers while listening to the radio. I know that today this might not seem a very exciting thing to do, but when I was younger, we enjoyed the more simple things in life.

Uncle Eddie had diabetes, and since we did not have much money at the time, he seldom ever visited a doctor. He ate and drank anything he wished and eventually it all caught up with him. One evening as we were all sitting at the kitchen table, he complained about something clouding his vision. In just a few days he began to see less and less in his right eye, until he totally lost his sight. When he eventually did visit the doctor, the news was bad. He was told that his loss of sight was due to his diabetes.

After losing his sight, Uncle Eddie's personality began to change. He became depressed and spent nights lying awake in his bed. He knew that things could only get worse as the days progressed. He was unable to properly care for his disease, and the result was that his body was seriously suffering. His family and friends attempted many times to help him with his depression, but he knew that his life would be cut short.

I remember the few times I caught him sitting at the side of his bed, and just staring into space. I felt so very sad for my uncle. Soon his right foot became infected, and the infection rapidly spread. He was taken to a Phoenix hospital and when the doctor saw the condition of his foot, he decided to amputate it that very day. So now my uncle was without sight in one eye, and without a right foot. When we returned home with Uncle Eddie, his depression got a lot worse. He now was fully aware of the seriousness of his condition and began to talk about death more and more.

Uncle Eddie called two of his friends over to the house one day, and informed them and my parents what he wished his funeral preparations to be. Thinking back, I know this was a healthy way to look at death and to prepare for it, but I was so very sad to think that my uncle would soon not be with me much longer. Everyone present said that they would do as he wished to fulfill his desires, but one of his wishes really scared us.

He said that he always had a great fear of being buried alive.

He wanted to make sure that he was completely dead when his coffin was lowered into the earth. To make sure of this he wanted to personally speak to the undertaker in Florence and to tell him about his unusual request. Uncle Eddie wrote a letter, which he and the undertaker signed. In the letter, Uncle Eddie had requested that right before his body was to be placed in the coffin, his heart would be pierced with a needle to make sure he was completely dead. This unusual agreement was signed and given to the local doctor, who placed the letter in his medical file.

As the months came and went, we all saw my uncle grow worse until one morning he did not wake up from his sleep. Uncle Eddie had died that night. The funeral arrangements were made, and just as he had requested, the undertaker pierced his still heart with a needle. The doctor was called to witness and sign his name, thereby stating that the procedure had been completed.

When the funeral and eventual burial took place, it was attended by all my uncle'S friends and relatives. We all deeply grieved for my uncle. His death affected me the most because, I fell into a pattern of crying myself to sleep each night with his image on my mind. It was terrible, I really took it hard.

About a month after my uncle's death, my whole family began to experience strange things in our house. My mother was the first person to hear her brother's presence in the house. One early morning, as she was sitting in the living room, she heard his familiar coughing and sneezing! As she tells it, "I felt that someone was in the living room with me. Then I heard the coughing sound coming from his room. I made the sign of the cross and walked towards my brother's bedroom and right before I entered it, I heard him sneeze! I opened the door, the room was empty. I sat down on his bed and cried and cried." After my mother's experience, I too had my own encounter with my uncle's spirit.

The following night as I lay asleep in my bed, I suddenly awoke with a feeling of over-whelming urgency. I don't know what this feeling was about, but I lay there in my bed for a few minutes just staring up at the ceiling. Eventually, I decided to go to the bathroom. As I returned to my bedroom, I walked past the living room

"We all deeply grieved for my uncle."

and froze in my steps. There, sitting on the couch, was my uncle! In the darkness, I clearly saw him as he put on one boot and then another. He must have sensed me watching him because he turned to me and gave me a little wave of his hand. I was filled with fear, and then my eyes filled with tears. I stood in place, then he disappeared. I screamed out, "Uncle Eddie don't go, please don't go!" My parents came to me, and through my tears I tried to tell them what I had just seen. We all broke down and cried that night.

Since that night, we did not experienced anything strangE until the following year. On the first anniversary of my uncle's death we held a remembrance rosary-prayer ceremony at the local church. That evening when we returned home from church, we all witnessed the strangest thing. As my family and I were seated at the kitchen table, we noticed that the single light bulb, hanging from an electrical cord in the middle of the kitchen ceiling, began to move! First it swung back and forth, then it began to make small circles. We all stopped our conversation and stared with open mouths at this odd behavior. Then I said, "It's my uncle, I know it's my uncle doing this!" Then the bulb began to immediately make even larger circles. The light and shadows were spinning all around us. We instinctively took hold of each others hands and began to pray.

The bulb began to spin even faster until we could hear it hit against the ceiling with each spin. I was afraid that it was going to break at any second. Then just as suddenly as it began its spinning, the bulb came to a complete stop. We all looked at each other as my mother prayed even louder. Each of us knew that the spirit of my uncle had caused this, and when my mother ended her prayer, she asked out loud, "Eddie, please be at peace and go to heaven. We are very scared and want you to have peace. Please go now, please." Nothing else happened that night.

Since then my family and I have not had another ghostly experience in the house. I personally believe that my uncle wanted to just let us know that he was still around. After mother told him that we wanted him to leave, he felt satisfied and did leave. I don't know what else to think about all of this. I know that my Uncle Eddie did not want to scare us like he did. I just hope he is finally at peace.

GLOBE

Globe, in east central Arizona, has been an important copper mining center for more than a century. Located in a steep canyon, at 3,500 feet, in the Pinal Mountains, Globe is the county seat of Gila County.

Globe was founded as a mining town in 1876 because of ample water and its attractive location for distribution of mining products. The city was incorporated twice prior to its present incorporation in 1907.

More than 20 percent of the employment in Globe is related to mining and production of copper. Over half of Gila County's sizable manufacturing sector employment is in copper smelting, refining, or rod production. In the area, there are three copper mines, several concentrators, a smelter, and a rod mill. All of Gila County is a designated Enterprise Zone.

The local tourism industry has been enhanced by a $50 million investment by the federal government to provide recreational campgrounds and amenities at nearby Roosevelt Lake.

Roxanne Moses' Story

I interviewed Roxanne-or Roxy-, at her ranch, located in a small canyon not far from Lake Roosevelt. Roxanne, her husband, and 46-six year old son have lived in this home all their lives. The house and land belonged to Roxanne's grandparents. Because of the distant location of their home, the Moses family rarely ventures out to town these days. Today, the family farms a few acres of cotton and ranches cattle.

The geography of the land is very dry, with a few groves of trees dotting the landscape. Some of the trees were planted by Roxanne's grandparents, and these can usually be identified by a partially standing wooden fence that meanders near the base of each tree. Years ago, the purpose of this fencing was to discourage the cattle from eating the sapling trees.

On the property are two large barns, several small sheds for tools and supplies, a chicken coop, two corrals, an out-house (no longer in use), the remains of a collapsed small house which was built at the turn of the century, and the main house.

Roxy has plenty of stories to tell about years past, but it is her story of the strange, ghostly things that she and her family have experienced on the ranch, that is most interesting indeed.

Like my own grandparents, homesteaders came to this part of the state to work in the copper mines and ranch. Many years ago when my own grandparents moved to this area to ranch and raise a family, Globe was just a small developing town. It turned out that fortune was on their side because on our particular piece of land, two springs were located on the property. while the property was remote, the availability of water was most important at the time.

To the east of the main house that grandfather built are the remains of the original house of the previous family that lived here. I don't know anything about those folks except that I understand they had a very hard time making a living. In the rubble of that house, my grandmother found a broken sewing machine, a small box of odds and ends, and pictures of people she believed were the original owners of the property. Grandfather won the property from the original owner in two card games. I was told that during the first poker game, the owner of the property lost all his money. After losing the first game, grandfather gave the man the opportunity to win back his loss with another game. This time the stakes were higher. Having run out of money, the man put up his homestead as a wager against grandfather's wealth of silver and Mexican gold coins.

It was with the loss of this last card game that Grandfather won the property. That's how things used to be done in those years. You could walk into a saloon and walk out a rich man or poor man; it all depended on who held the lucky cards.

Grandfather now had a ranch and a bag of money he used to develop the land. My grandparents built the new house and barns, and soon my father was born. During 1917, the first year of my own life, grandmother died. Grandfather died two years after. I was the only child my parents had. I was quite lucky to have been born; My mother had three miscarriages before me. AS an only child, I was spoiled rotten. I didn't have any friends to play with because of the distance between the houses. However, we did go to church every Sunday, and that's when I would get to meet and play with the other children of my own age. The earliest memory I have of ghosts took place when I was a little girl.

I remember one night looking out my window, I spotted mysterious small balls of light that bounced and danced in the distant hills. My parents also saw the lights. Mother and Father told me that the lights were caused by the spirits of the Apaches who used to inhabit the hills and canyons around here. The lights; appeared and disappeared at all times of the year. I was never afraid of these lights; we all just accepted them as something normal. To this day the lights can still be seen.

Aside from these lights,is another, more frightening thing I have seen several times on the ranch. One day when I was about 19 years old, I was moving three horses from one corral to another. This was during the late morning, just before noon.

"These hills are filled with snakes...."

Suddenly the animals began to act strangely. Something was spooking them to run. I thought that there might be a rattlesnake nearby, a cougar or something. These hills are filled with snakes, and it is not unusual for them to be found close to the house. One evening I spotted five of them coiled up next to our front door!

I walked over to the barn and looked everywhere. There wasn't a snake or anything else anywhere. Still, when I tried to corral the horses by moving them through the area, they once again put their ears back—as a scared horse does—and refused to pass by the barn. This time when I glanced over to the opened barn door, I spotted a strange man standing beside the door holding on to a horse's harnessES. I was not familiar with either this man or his horse. I immediately got a weird feeling about them both.

The man was dressed in a peculiar manner, wearing waidh-high dark brown trousers, which were held up with thick black leather suspenders. His shirt was greyish in color, and he sported a long thick moustache. I waved to him. He ignored me. Then he and the horse turned around and walked into the barn. I was annoyed by his lack of manners and walked over to speak to him.

As I entered the barn, the man and horse were nowhere to be found! I thought to myself, "What happened? Was I going crazy?" Then it hit me like a slap on the face. I had just seen a ghost! I ran out of that barn so fast, I must have flown like a bird! I tell you I was scared! When I got inside the house, I told my mother about what I had just seen. I was so excited and WAS going on and on about the ghost. Mother just sat in her chair and listened. Soon, I got a little upset with her calm atti-tude and asked her why didn't she get as excited as I was? She told me to calm down and to listen to what she had to say.

She said, "Oh, Roxy, I've seen ghosts here several times before. I just haven't told you about them because I didn't want to scare you."

I was so surprised to hear my mother's words. I said to her, "Why, why didn't you Trust me enough to tell me about them?"

My mother responded, "Well, because look at how you are reacting to what you just saw. Now how do you think you would have reacted if I had told you about my and your father's experiences?"

I answered, "You mean Father also has seen ghosts?"

"Oh, yes, honey. Several times!" she said. I was too surprised for words. After a few minutes, we went into the living room, and Mother began to tell me her story about her encounter with the ghosts. "You know those old pictures that grandmother found in the old house? Well, I've seen the woman in one of those pictures, and so has your father!"

"You know those old pictures that grandmother found in the old house, well...."

She said that about the time that I was 5 years of age, she had her first encounter with a ghost in the house. We had all gone to sleep for the night, and sometime after midnight, a noise awoke her from her sleep. She opened her eyes and saw a light coming from the living room. Thinking that my father had left a lamp on, she got out of bed to investigate. As she entered the living room, she stopped dead in her steps. There standing at the door that led to my bedroom was a woman whom my mother did not immediately recognize. The woman must have been about 60 years old and was wearing a long black dress of Victorian style. Mother noticed that the woman's hair was parted in the middle, and pulled back tightly into a large bun.

Suddenly, something within mother told her that this woman was a ghost. Even more surprising was when mother recognized the woman from pictures she had seen among the pictures discovered in the collapsed house years before!

Mother said that as soon as she realized who this ghost was, she raised her hands to her bosom and calmly spoke to the ghost saying, "I know you are a ghost. Why did you come to our house?" The ghost woman reached for the long silver chain which hung around her neck, at the end of which was a black, flat shiny stone. The ghost did not respond to my mother's question. Instead, the ghost slowly turned her head to one side and gradually began to fade from view.

Slowly, she disappeared completely into thin air! Mother said that instead of being frightened, she was mostly fascinated by actually having seen a real ghost! You would have to know my mother to know why she would have such a reaction. She WAS not a very timid woman by any definition!

After the ghost disappeared, mother went into my bedroom and made sure that I was asleep and that no harm had come to me. Satisfied, knowing I was safe, she went back to bed. The following morning she informed my father about her experience. Dad's reaction was disbelief. Mother said, "I don't care what you think. I saw what I saw, and that's good enough for me!" Little did my father know that very soon his disbelief was to change.

A few nights after my mother's experience, father was in the barn finishing up with the day's work. It was late, and there was no electricity in the barn, so kerosene lamps were used for light. Father had two lamps lit in the area where he was rubbing a saddle with oil. He said that he heard the sound of footsteps crunching down upon small stones on the dirt floor. The footsteps got closer as they made their way towards him in the darkness.

Thinking it was my mother, he turned to look in the direction of the footsteps. Standing directly a few yards in front of my father, was the same woman whom my mother had described to him just a few nights before! The woman was holding a lit candle. My father—being the brave man that he is!—let out a scream and threw the small can of oil he was holding at the ghost! He ran to the house and told my mother about the ghost woman in the barn. As they both returned to the barn to investigate, they found it empty.

The next morning my father discovered on the dirt floor in the barn, drops of beeswax, which had dripped in the same area where the woman with her lit candle was standing! To be sure, this made a quick believer of my father. No more would he doubt the existence of ghosts!

Sadly, both my parents have since died. My son has been the only other person who has had an encounter with a ghost on the property. His experience took place after he returned home from the army in the late '70s one day, he was writing a letter as he sat under one of the large trees by the house.

He said that he heard a noise in the tree's branches above him, and as he looked up, a flock of birds came down from the tree and began to fly all about him. This was definitely unusual behavior for birds. The birds actually flew down in a mass horde. They did not hurt him in any way; they just were flying weirdly all about him.

Being concerned about the bird's reaction, he got up and moved under another tree. The birds flew away into the distant hills. Apparently, that was not the end of it, because what ever invisible force had directed the birds, the same force followed my son to this new location.

As he picked up his pen, and again tried to write, suddenly he felt an invisible hand give the side of his face a big slap, and off flew his glasses! At the same time, he heard the sound of a woman's laughter! He looked all around and saw no one. That was enough for him. He walked over to pick up his glasses, and ran quickly over to the center of the yard. His arms were covered in goose bumps! He wanted to get as far away from the trees as possible. He knew there was no rational way to explain what he had just experienced, except to believe that it had to be a ghost.

Well, as of this day we have not had any further experiences with the ghosts of the man and his horse, or of the woman. We all believe that the ghosts must be of the family who lived here before us. It is clear to my husband and me that the woman we saw is the same one in the old picture as my mother had seen. Aside from my own son's experience with being hit on the side of his head, no one else has been attacked. Now that my husband and I are much older, I don't think the ghosts want to be bothering with us seniors. I guess they think that we'll soon be joining them, so why bother.

HOLBROOK

Holbrook is on the banks of the Little Colorado River in northeastern Arizona's Navajo County high plateau country.

In 1881 railroad tracks were laid in northeastern Arizona, passing through an area known as Horsehead Crossing. The following year, a railroad station was built at Horsehead Crossing and the community's name was changed to Holbrook in honor of Henry Randolph Holbrook, first chief engineer of the Atlantic and Pacific Railroad. Holbrook, at an elevation of 5,080 feet, became the county seat of Navajo County in 1895 and was incorporated in 1917.

Holbrook is an important trade center for northeastern Arizona. Its location on historic Route 66 and on Interstate 40 at the junction of four major highways, between the Apache Sitgreaves National Forest to the south and the Navajo and Hopi Indian Reservations to the north, makes tourism important to the local economy.

Roger Bowen's Story

The interview for Roger's story took place at a local restaurant. We sat in a booth in the back of this hang-out, and after ordering two

67

cups of coffee, the interview began.

Roger is a man of 66 years, and except for the five years he spent in Viet Nam and the two years he spent married to his ex-wife in Arkansas, he has lived in the small town of Holbrook for most of his life. Three years ago, he divorced his ex-wife when he discovered she was already married to another man in Arkansas. As soon as his divorce was finalized, he returned to Arizona and now owns and operates a vending machine company, which ser-vices Holbrook and the neighbor-ing towns.

Roger is a man who knows his community very well. He cur-rently lives in a two-bedroom home about three miles outside of town, which gives him the quiet and privacy he said he needs. Roger also enjoys traveling, and on occasion travels a couple hundred miles west, to the city of Las Vegas, Nevada for a weekend of "slots."

Roger stated, "You know, I've seen a lot of things, but what I experienced with my folks here in Holbrook just about did it for me." What follows is Mr. Bowen's experience with a sad ghost in Hol-brook.

My family consisted of my parents and an older sister, who was two years my senior. We lived on five acres just east of town, off highway 180. There was nothing really special about our house and property. We were not rich or anything, but because we had some farm animals, and because my father did a little farming, we always had something to eat. Just above the hill from us lived another family. They had three little kids-two boys and a baby girl. I was about 19 years old when this whole ghost thing began.

It started one day when our neighbor's wife came over to our house. At about 4 pm there was a knock at our front door. My sister opened it, and there stood the neighbor's wife who we could tell was quite shaken up about something. She asked to speak with my mother. My mother and the woman sat outside on the porch and talked. My sister and I stayed in the house with our ears pressed to the closed front door. We could hear the neighbor explain to my mother how the neighbor's husband, in a drunken rage, had thrown her against a wall in their bedroom. There was more to the story, but it was so long ago that I've forgotten most of what she said. This is how things began to develop terribly with the neighbors, to the point that things started to get more violent.

One late evening, there was another knock at our front door. When I opened it, there on our front porch stood the wife, but this time she was holding a bloody towel to her face. Her husband had taken a swing at her and hit her nose. My father drove her to the doctor in town and luckily for her, her nose was not broken. However, it did leave her with nasty looking black eyes and swollen face.

I know it might sound strange, but years ago it was not considered neighborly to get involved in a neighbors personal problems. The last thing my father wanted to do was to have bad blood with a neighbor. So, all my mother could do was comfort the poor woman with words. It was not long after that incident that the worst happened.

I remember the time that my father and I were cleaning out the stall where we milked our cow. After shoveling out all the dirty straw, I asked my father to pass me a fresh bale of straw to

"Mother and sister were outside looking in the direction of our neighbors house."

spread over the floor of the stall. As my arms reached to take the bale from his hands, right at that second, we heard the gunshot. We stopped what we were doing and ran to our house. My mother and sister were outside looking in the direction of our neighbor's house. When we reached our house, my mother asked my father if we also had heard the gunshot. As we both began to answer my mother's question, we heard in the distance the crying sound of the neighbors' two young boys. We knew then at that instant that something awful had taken place. We all quickly walked to the neighbors' house, increasing our pace as the boys' cries got louder and louder. We didn't know what to expect.

When we entered the front yard, the front door was open wide, and one of the boys was crying out, "My mother is all bloody." Soon after we found the husband sitting on the living room floor holding his younger son and crying to himself. It did not take us long to discover the reason for the sadness. The wife had minutes before taken a shotgun into her bedroom and placed the barrel to her chest and pulled the trigger. Apparently she had taken enough of her husband's beatings and had decided that the only way out of her living hell was to end her own life. I cannot begin to describe the blood and smell that hit us when we entered that room!

The authorities soon were called, and the investigation ruled the tragedy a suicide. The father was taken away for questioning and was soon let go. In the meantime, my parents had volunteered to care for the children until the father returned.

When he did return, he piled the kids into his car with a few clothes, and off they went to live with his parents. The father never again set foot on his property or home. A few days later, we saw a truck with a trailer drive up to the property. The two men filled the truck bed and trailer with most of the family's furniture. They finished their work in just a few hours, then off they drove. All was over and done with, so we thought.

My mother never really got over her neighbor's death. The memories of that tragic day also weighed heavy on my sister. We were all pretty sad during the months that followed. It was difficult to forget, because each time we went out our door, the neighbor's house was visible just above the hill. Damn, it was sad.

One day, about six months after the tragedy, my curiosity got the better of me, and I decided to take a walk over to the house. I took my dog with me, and slowly walked up the short hill. Reaching the back door, I just stood there staring at the back yard, thinking about the two children that used to play there. I have to admit that I was a bit uncomfortable. It was midday, and the sun was hot and shining bright. I guess the sun gave me the courage to reach for the door knob and slowly turn it until it clicked open.

My dog, began to bark as if something was inside the house. This made me nervous, but I opened the door anyway and slowly walked inside. There were clothes and a few toys thrown about. The refrigerator door was left open, and mice had made nests under the kitchen cabinets. Their droppings were everywhere.

Suddenly, I felt a cold chill come over me. My dog took off like a flash! I wanted to do the same, but then I began to feel an unexplainable dizziness take over. I tried to open my

"Something" was inside the house."

mouth and to move my legs, but I was unable to. I fell to the floor, and boy, let me tell you, was I scared! I didn't faint, I just remained on the floor for a few minutes, shaking with such a chill. I finally did manage to prop myself upright when suddenly my eyes were drawn to the bedroom door, which was about 10 feet away.

There in the doorway was the figure of a person! I was not able to make out any details of a woman or man, but I knew it was a person. I was so scared. I tried to move, but I just could not do it. As I watched the figure, it became clearer and clearer that it was the ghost of the wife. I called out to her, "Please don't hurt me. I'm sorry! Please don't hurt me!" Her staring eyes never left me. She just stared as if waiting for me to make a move or to say something more. I sat in that position crying loudly. Then, adjusting her position from one foot to the other, she turned her body away from me and walked into the bedroom.

As soon as she disappeared from my view, I found the strength to rise from my seated position and get out of that house! I can remember that day very clearly. I'll never forget it, never! I've only told just a few people about this. Some people just don't believe that such a thing could actually happen. I don't know how to prove this.

I hope that poor woman is finally resting in her grave, and

that her ghost stays with the Lord. I don't think it should be mingling with the living. You know what they say: "A person who dies by his or her own hands will never find rest."

The Navajo County Courthouse

This historic courthouse is located at the northeast corner of Arizona Street and Navajo Boulevard. Currently within its walls are located the Chamber of Commerce offices and the Historical Society Museum. In 1976 a new governmental center was established south of the city. All county offices were then moved from the courthouse to this new location. In 1981 the County Board of Supervisors requested that the Navajo County Historical Society open a museum in the old building. Local residents graciously donated furniture, keepsakes and other wonderful items along with written family histories to include in the displays which are currently on view in the museum.

Aside from the many notorious trials that were held in the courtroom, only one hanging took place, in the courtyard on January 8, 1900, at 2 p.m.. The name of the executed was George Smiley who was hung for the murder of T. J. McSweeney.

Holbrook, Arizona, *Dec 1st 1899*

Mr. *X B Berryhill*

You are hereby cordially invited to attend the hanging of one

George Smiley, Murderer.

His soul will be swung into eternity on ~~January~~ *Dec* 8, ~~1900~~ *1899*

at 2 o'clock, p. m., sharp.

Latest improved methods in the art of scientific strangulation will be employed and everything possible will be done to make the proceedings cheerful and the execution a success.

F. J. WATTRON,
Sheriff of Navajo County.

Invitations to the hanging of George Smiley, for murder, which occurred at Holbrook on January 8, 1900. Issued by F. J. Wattron, Sheriff of Navajo County.

This first invitation, the news of which was sent out by the Associated Press, brought a letter of condemnation from then President William McKinley to Governor Nathan Oakes Murphy, of the Territory of Arizona. Governor Murphy severely rebuked Sheriff Wattron, and issued a stay of execution, whereupon the Sheriff sent out the second sarcastic invitation

Revised Statutes of Arizona, Penal Code, Title X., Section 1848, Page 807, makes it obligatory on Sheriff to issue invitations to executions. form (unfortunately) not prescribed.

Holbrook, Arizona, *Jan. 5th* 1900.

Mr. *A. B. Weterjhill*

    With feelings of profound sorrow and regret, I hereby invite you to attend and witness the private, decent and humane execution of a human being; name, George Smiley; crime, murder.

    The said George Smiley will be executed on January 8, 1900, at 2 o'clock p. m.

    You are expected to deport yourself in a respectful manner, and any "flippant" or "unseemly" language or conduct on your part will not be allowed. Conduct, on anyone's part, bordering on ribaldry and tending to mar the solemnity of the occasion will not be tolerated.

                         F. J. WATTRON,
                               Sheriff of Navajo County.

I would suggest that a committee, consisting of Governor Murphy, Editors Dunbar, Randolph and Hull, wait on our next legislature and have a form of invitation to executions embodied in our Laws.

Marita R. Keams' Story

I interviewed Marita at the courthouse, where she is currently employed as receptionist and information clerk for the Museum and Chamber of Commerce. Marita is a Navajo woman who has had numerous encounters with ghosts at the courthouse. She believes that perhaps one of the spirits that follows her around the property is the ghost of the executed man Smiley. "I know he's around here all the time I can feel him looking at me."

Marita R. Keams

What follows is a detailed account of something that cannot be contained behind glass cases or roped off in rooms. When the lights are turned off at the Navajo County Courthouse and all daily business has ended, another type of activity is just beginning to stir, an activity of curiously weird noises, voices, and more.

Marita can tell you what she has experienced, but of course the true challenge is to experience these eerie events for yourself. The museum's hours are 8 a.m. to 5 p.m.

I've been working at the courthouse for three years, and before that I was working at the Petrified Forest National Park gift shop. I have had numerous experiences with the ghosts in the building, and I also know of others who have experienced strange things first hand.

My experiences gave me the impression that I was not welcomed in the building. I guess I was being tested. Being a Navajo, we are taught that if you keep any possessions of the deceased—a shirt, furniture or whatever—the spirit of the dead person will attach itself to the item, and you might have some trouble on your hands.

In the museum, there are lots of items of the past that are displayed in the showcases such as old Indian grinding stones, arrows, clothing, as well as lots of non-Indian items. The museum director has informed me that some of these items that have been securely locked behind glass cases have been strangely found outside of these cases, and placed in other locations by "someone." Our museum's kitchen display seems to attract most of the activity. Utensils and other items are rearranged to fit an unseen person's own whim for order. A museum employee named Jane refuses to open any of the display cases unless someone is with her. She keeps her own experiences to herself. Interestingly enough, our own museum director is hesitant to be alone in the building.

All our employees have experienced our names being called out from the second floor. In my case, I heard a friendly female voice, but others have heard both male and female voices calling them when they are alone in the courthouse. Another employee who was the past city tourism director had quite an experience of his own.

His experience happened while he and his family were driving past the courthouse one night. As they drove by the museum, he noticed that the lights were left on in the second floor, when they should have been turned off. He drove his car to the rear of the building and informed his wife and teenage son that he would return after finding out who was in the courthouse at such a late hour. He opened the back door and just as he was about to enter, his wife called out to him from the car that there was a woman on the stairs on the second floor landing, looking out the window at them. He returned to the car, and sure enough, there was a woman whom he did not recognize staring at them. He, his wife and son entered the building and searched for the strange woman. Although they did a thorough search, they never found her.

Just a few months after I began working here, a group of kids took a Ouija board up to the third floor on a Halloween night, and apparently made contact with a ghost of the building. The ghost identified himself as "George." George was the person who was hanged right outside the courthouse in 1900.

I was alone one evening in the courthouse when suddenly, I heard a loud, banging metal sound coming from the second floor. As loud as it was, I was not about to go upstairs by myself and investigate. I just remained where I was, hearing the sound. The next day, I asked co-workers about the sound, and he

"Suddenly, the footsteps started up once more!"

said, "Oh, that happens now and then." I decided not to inquire any further.

Just a few months after my first experience, I was once more in the building after locking up for the day. It was dark, and I was on the second floor standing next to a window. Suddenly, I began to hear the sound of someone walking down the staircase from the third floor approaching the second floor where I was. The doors were locked, and I wasn't sure who this stranger might be. The thought crossed my mind that I could be in danger. As I kept quiet and listened for the footsteps, I noticed that they stopped.

Trying to be as quiet as possible, I listened for any sound at all. There was no further noise coming from the stairs. I convinced myself that perhaps my mind was playing tricks on me- after all, I had heard others speak about the courthouse being haunted. Maybe this was just my crazy imagination. Suddenly, the footsteps started up once more! I carefully made my way to the opened door and peered out looking onto the staircase. I saw no one. I realized that I must be experiencing something ghostly. I sure didn't want to stay in the building any longer. I quickly walked down the stairs, grabbed my purse and keys, and shot out the front door!

There is another event I have experienced several times during the winter: doors opening and closing on their own. Once I

"The feeling is strongest in the room where the chuck wagon is displayed."

even witnessed the door knob of the front door of the courthouse turn, and then the door opened and closed. We have double doors that are located directly behind the front desk, which lead out to the rear of the building. I once heard these doors swing open. I walked to the doors to investigate the reason for the noise, and I found that the doors were locked just as I had left them.

Besides my own experiences, public visitors to the courthouse have on numerous times approached the front desk to tell of experiencing cold chills or that they feel that someone is following them. As the visitors, I have also experienced these same feelings. It feels like a blanket of very cold air is passing right through me. I know this sounds strange, but I'm also not the only one that has experienced this. I have been told by visitors that the room where this feeling is strongest is in the room where an old chuck wagon is displayed. I was very surprised to have heard this because that is exactly the room where I have always felt the same thing happen to me.

Another strange unexplained thing that continues to happen in the courthouse are that the faucets in the men's room seem to be turned on by an invisible hand. At the end of the day, I thoroughly check every corner of the courthouse, making sure that everything is as it is supposed to be. There have been several instances when I'll return after checking the men's room and find that the faucets have been turned on. I don't know who could have done this, asI was the only person in the building. I have a suspicion that it is the ghost of "George."

I remember another day when I was seated at the front desk,and the greeting card rack began to turn, then abruptly stop. I thought that there might be a small child behind it who was having fun spinning the rack. I rose from my chair and walked over to have a closer look; there was no one near it!

There was a time when for several nights after leaving the building, I would feel the presence of someone following me to the parking lot and into my car. I felt the usual cold chills, and this presence would not leave me. I would even take frequent glances at my rear view mirror hoping to spot something in the back seat.

At other times, I'll feel the invisible hand of someone playing with my hair. I have felt my body being touched so many times that I chose not to discuss this with anyone anymore. They might think I'm crazy. There are times when I'll be so annoyed with George's behavior that I'll yell out, "George, please stop doing this!" I won't experience any more activity for several days afterward, so I know he is paying attention to my anger.

Once we had a man come to us as a volunteer. This guy was ordered by the traffic court to do community work at the museum as a part of his sentence. Our employee's first impression of this volunteer was not a very positive one. This guy had heard some of the stories about our ghosts, and when he arrived for work, he began to make fun of George and openly state that he was not afraid of ghosts. We didn't trust this worker and didn't want to leave him alone in the building unsupervised. In the museum, we have a donation box and a few small, valuable things in the gift shop that would not be very difficult to steal. Well, one day I asked him to bring me some brochures from the rear of the building, where the old jail cells are located. We now use these original cells as storage areas for office supplies. Just a few seconds after he left, I heard him scream. He came running to me, saying that the bars and metal were making loud noises and the ghosts were trying to get him. I just smiled and giggled when he told me this. I knew that "our George" was keeping an eye on this guy.

The following is the deposition of T. J. McSweeney after being shot. Filed on October 4, 1899.

"I knew that "our George" was keeping an eye on this guy."

Question: What is your name?
Answer: T. J. McSweeney.
Question: Where do you reside?
Answer: Have been residing at Dennison.
Question: You are employed as section foreman of the Santa Fe Pacific Railroad Company at Dennison?
Answer: Yes, sir, at Dennison.
Question: What is the man's name who did the shooting?
Answer: George Smiley.
Question: What do you think caused him to commit this act? What were his reasons?
Answer: He claimed I ought to give him time check when he quit. I had to go to El Paso to have my wife's eyes treated and I asked Mr. Crowley to send man down there and this fellow worked one day for Garrity

and then quit and then, of course, Garrity was the man to give him his time check. I had no more to do with it.

Question: He worked for Mr. Garrity after you had taken leave?

Answer: Yes, sir.

Question: Go ahead and tell me just what he said?

Answer: He just walked right up to me and either said, "Give me my time check" or "I want my time check," but before I had a chance to reply, came right up and struck me.

Question: What did he strike you with?

Answer: I do not know; something hard.

Question: Where did he hit you?

Answer: In the mouth and face; just one blow.

Question: What did you do then?

Answer: I started to run and he shot me in the back and I kept running.

JEROME

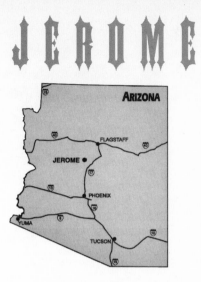

Jerome was once a roaring mining town with 15,000 people and multi-storied buildings and fine homes. It was incorporated in 1899, but with the fall of copper prices and the closing of the Phelps Dodge Mine in 1953, it became the world's largest "ghost city."

In the foothills of central Arizona's Verde Valley, surrounded by the Prescott National Forest, the town is at an altitude of 5,248 feet.

Jerome produced over a billion dollars worth of copper, gold, silver and zinc in its 70-year active life. Today, life is quite different. The town was designated a National Historical Landmark in 1967. Its economy is now based on tourism and recreation. Antique, craft and gift shops, small boutiques, and art galleries are located in the once-deserted stores along Main Street. Jerome also has one of Arizona's oldest saloon-style bars.

Jerome State Historic Park, "down the hill" from the center of town, features the former Douglas Mansion which has been converted into a museum with exhibits on the area's history. Jerome Historical Society Mine Museum, on Main Street, exhibits ore collections and mining equipment of the past. The annual Paso De Casas (Home Tour) celebrations are held the

third weekend in May.
Other attractions include
Traveling Jail, Gold King
Mine, Big Pit, and United
Verde Extension Mines.

History of The Spirit Room

The Conner building was constructed in 1898. The bar was
smaller than it is today and, when built, a portion of the bar was
used as the lobby for the rented rooms on the top floor. The
local prostitutes, or "soiled doves" of the evening, did not use
the rooms for their "profession" because the rooms were too
expensive. At the west end of the building was a false storefront
that opened into a alleyway known as "husband's alley." This
became the area where the "working girls" would ply their
vocation. Today, that area is long gone.

The bar as well has gone through some changes. At one time
it was a smoke shop, then a restaurant, then a freight office, and
today, once more, a bar renamed, "The Spirit Room."

Paul Milvski's Story

I have been the owner of the
The Spirit Room bar for five
years. For a time, I lived in
Seattle, Washington. I owned
a civil engineering firm, which
I grew tired of. I had been visiting Jerome for some 15 years,
and one day when the bar was

Paul Milvski

put up for sale, the thought hit me to purchase it. So I did.

When I first moved to Jerome, I rented a room upstairs in room number 2. I lived there for a few months before I actually opened the bar. People in town had their stories about ghosts being in the building. They even came forward to explain to me about what they had seen and felt. Some even said that they had been touched by the ghosts of the building! I was told to be on the look-out for the ghost of a woman in room number 1. Apparently, there is a woman in a

red dress who appears to peo-ple. The room is located directly above the main entrance to the bar. When she appears, she just stands there looking at you without making a sound and then slowly disap-pears.

An artist who once stayed in room number 1 painted the large mural that can be seen today above the bar. He said that he painted the image of the ghost woman in a red dress that kept appearing to him in his dreams.

I've also been told that room number 5 was filled with "strange goings on." In that room people might experience temperature differences, hot and cold spots, the hair on their arms standing straight up, etc.

I have heard cracking sounds and other such noises on the second floor that have kept me up all night. I have also experienced what I would call "odd, strange feelings" in the building. Other than that, I have not personally had anything else happen to me. Haven't seen a thing. Honest, nothing more. Yep, that's it, nothing else. Not a thing.

History of The Grand Hotel

The Jerome Grand Hotel, a National Historic Landmark, was built in 1926. Formerly the United Verde Hospital, it opened in January 1927 and was one of the most modern hospitals in the Western States. It served the Town of Jerome and the surrounding communities until its closing in 1950. The Hospital was kept in standby condition, fully furnished, equipped, and ready to reopen, if needed until the 1970s. It was purchased in 1994 from the Phelps Dodge Mining Company to be historically renovated and reopened as Van-Alan's Jerome Grand Hotel in 1996.

Despite over three years of renovation, the building has maintained over 95% of its original integrity. The Otis elevator is once again providing service to all five levels, and heat for the hotel is provided by the original Kewanee boiler system installed in 1926.

As one of the highest public buildings in the Verde Valley, (elevation 5,260 feet), Panoramic views of the San Francisco

Peaks, the Red Rocks of Sedona and the entire Verde Valley are breathtaking. The hotel is located within walking distance of Downtown Jerome.

Along with the hotel and gift shop, the historically renovated 1920's style lounge and restaurant are now open making the Jerome Grand Hotel the only full-service hotel in Jerome in over 40 years.

The death of Claude M. Harvey

On April 4, 1935, *The Prescott Evening Courier* reported that Claude M. Harvey, an employee of the United Verde Hospital and a well-known resident of Jerome, was instantly killed in the basement of the hospital. The man's unavoidable death was caused when his head was pinned under the elevator. Further, there were no eye-witnesses to the tragedy.

Born in Scotland on February 20, 1872, Mr. Harvey had been employed as the hospital's fireman engineer from 1932 until his death. Mr. Harvey was known to the community of Jerome simply as "Scotty" or "Dad."

John Zivkovich, a hospital employee discovered the body. Dr. M.S. Meade examined the body, and Mr. T. C. Henson, electrical engineer, removed Mr. Harvey's body from the accident scene and testified that the elevator was in perfect working order.

Given all the testimonies following the death, presented to the coroner's jury, there were many individuals, then as now, who believe that Scotty Harvey was murdered. Various theories of the possible crime exist among present employees of the hotel and townsfolk. These circulated stories lead the listener to wonder if Scotty's ghost is not yet resting in peace. Could the shadowy figure of a short man, seen darting about the hallways and boiler room of the present hotel, be the ghost of Scotty?

Could the presence that is sensed of a man on the second and third floors of the hotel be that same spirit?

Elin Heard's Story

Elin Heard

I'm originally from Wales and am the bar manager of the Grand View Lounge. Prior to working at the hotel, I was told about scary things that had taken place in the building.

My only experience with a ghost took place right here in the bar of the Grand View Lounge. As I was entering the lounge one day, I saw a fellow worker standing behind the bar. Strangely, standing directly behind her was a woman whom I did not recognize. The strange woman was not very old, about in her late 20s. She had long dark hair, pulled back, and was wearing a white blouse with a high collar. Over the blouse, she wore a dark jacket. My impression was that this woman was wearing clothing of a bygone time.

I soon could tell that this woman did not want me to notice her because as I began to stare at her, she quickly turned around and went through the doorway into the back storage room of the bar. There is no exit door in the storage room-just one way in and one way out.

I asked the employee, "What the heck is that woman doing here in the bar?"

The employee was perplexed at my question, because she responded with, "What woman? There's no one here." I told her that I had seen this woman standing right behind her and that she had just walked away into the storage room. The employee was speechless because she obviously did not see the woman.

I decided to investigate the storage room. When I did, I found no one in sight. I knew immediately that the strange woman I had just seen was a ghost. I have lived in a lot of places where ghosts are regularly seen. So I guess I accept such things and do not get very excited. I accept them for what they are, and I leave it at that.

I have not heard of other staff or guests seeing this spirit in the lounge. Some people might not wish to tell about such experiences you

"She quickly turned around and went through the doorway into the back storage room!"

know. However, one story in particular that I can recall is about a woman guest.

One evening, the woman removed her necklace and earrings and placed them on the table by her bed. After waking in the morning, she reached for her jewelry and discovered that her necklace and earrings had fused together into a clump of melted gold! I have also heard talk of a ghostly little boy, about the age of six or seven that appears on the third floor. He is seen with a playful grin on his face, and then he disappears.

Jennifer A. Edens's Story

I've been working at the hotel as the front desk clerk and gift shop cashier for over six months. Prior to working here, I definitely was told about the building being haunted. Growing up in the not-so-distant town of Sedona, local people were well aware of the hotel's ghostly reputation.

I consider myself to be a logical woman, and I have tried to make sense about what I have experienced here. I also know that what I have seen at the hotel is not normal and can't be explained in logical terms.

Jennifer A. Eden

My personal experiences did not take long—just a few weeks before I started my job. One evening I was alone, working the 4 pm-to-midnight shift. I was seated at the phone switchboard when I heard noise coming from the gift shop area.

I got up from my chair and went to investigate. I saw that several items which I had securely placed on the gift shop shelves now on the floor. An unseen force of some kind was actually tossing small dolls and other bric-a-brac off the shelves! The items that I had personally placed on the shelves went flying! Then everything stopped. I have not had this happen since.

"Sometimes I get the strange feeling that someone is watching me."

Once, I arranged the chairs in the sitting area directly in front of my desk, then turned my back. Moments later, they have been returned to their original position by an unseen hand. I know this might seem nutty, but I am the only person in the room, and this really does happen.

At night when I am seated behind the desk reading a book, I sometimes get the strange feeling that someone is watching me. I can "feel" the glaring eyes of a man staring at me from the stairs just a few feet away. Once, when this feeling became too overpowering, I quickly turned my head and looked toward the stairs. As I did this, I got a glimpse of a shadowy figure of a man! He stood still and then walked up the stairs and out of my sight. That shook me up a bit. I was quite alert throughout the rest of the night.

You might have heard about the employee, Mr. Harvey, who once worked at the building and who committed suicide? Some say he was murdered. Well, they found his body at the bottom of the elevator shaft which is just a few feet away from my working area. That sure gives me a lot of comfort knowing a dead man's body was found over there...

Once, as I walked down to the basement, I entered the boiler room and saw a shadowy figure of a man walking about the room. I didn't think much about this at the time, because I thought it was the manager of the hotel. I soon found out that the same day I was downstairs, the manager was out of town. The thought of encountering that ghost down there alone just sent shivers down my back. Eventually, the word got around about my boiler room experience, and other staff came forward to tell me about seeing

"I'll get calls from rooms that are empty!"

the same shadowy figure in other areas of the hotel. I know that there has got to be a reason for this ghost appearing to all of us. Could it be the spirit of the man that died here? Who can tell?

I have had another strange thing happen. My switchboard has received calls from rooms that are empty. This switchboard is an old one but works perfectly fine. I have never had any problem with the system. I began to get these unusual calls from rooms that have been vacated by a guest. Once when I checked out an elderly couple, from my window, I saw them get into their car and drive off. No sooner had they done this, the switchboard began to ring; the call was coming from the room they had just left. I carefully picked up my receiver and said, "Yes, can I help you?" All I heard was static at the other end. I felt as if someone was playing with me. The thought did cross my mind that perhaps it might be the maid playing a trick on me, but I know the maid and she would not do such a thing. At one time when the switchboard began to ring in an empty room, the maid walked right past my desk! It couldn't be the maid because she herself has experienced unusual ghostly things and I know that she has been so shaken up by these experiences, that she would not play around with me like that.

I hope I don't ever see anymore shadows or hear any more noises and ringing phones. I work the evening hours, and I don't need to be shaken when I am all alone.

Laina R. Galloway's Story

I have been working as head housekeeper of the hotel for seven months. I was born in Jerome and moved away for several years before returning. Growing up, I always heard local stories about the hotel being haunted, and one day I personally experienced strange events at the building for

Laina R. Galloway

myself. As a child, I lived with my family in a home just above the hill from the building that used to be a hospital before the present owners turned it into The Grand Hotel.

Well, one day my sister and I walked down the hill and outside of the building. Suddenly, we both clearly heard a woman's screams coming from within the abandoned building. The numerous stories that people used to tell were about screams and other noises coming from the old hospital. Now we were hearing them for ourselves. Of course, there could have been someone in the building playing a trick on us, but it all seemed so spontaneous and real at the time. Not wanting to investigate any further, we ran home.

A few days after I began my job at the hotel, I began to hear strange sounds coming from rooms I knew to be empty, the sound of people conversing with each other. Even now I get scared and uneasy when I recall that. My sister, who also works in housekeeping, has also heard the voices in other rooms. Most often we hear them on the third floor, in rooms 31 and 33, 39a and 39b. Those days, I get scared working alone in those rooms.

In one room I saw the strangest thing: a shadow of a man walked right past me! As soon as I entered the room, I began to see a hundred little lights floating around. It was as if they were  moving as a group in mid-air, much like a school of fishes might behave. The lights really appeared to be like someone had thrown handfuls of sparkles into the air. After a few seconds, they slowly disappeared.

Another time, while in a room, I heard the sound of an old,

large cart being wheeled across the hall. I could tell it was an old cart because of the squeaking sounds its metal wheels made. At the time I was using the hotel's only cart, and it was in the room with me. Curiosity got the better of me, so I walked into the hallway to investigate. The hallway was empty. Could that sound be the noise of a hospital cart, used years ago when the building was a hospital? Or could it have been a hospital cot being pushed by the ghost of a nurse?

Again alone in a room, I'll hear my name being called out. I'll turn and face the direction of the voice, and there will be no one. My sister has had this happen to her, but "they" actually scream out her name in her ear. Of course this upsets her, but what can she do?

I'll also have doors slam shut while I'm in a room. There is no wind to cause such a thing to happen, so what would cause closet and room doors to close with such force? Whenever a door slams on me, I loudly say, "Stop it and leave me alone! Can't you see I have to work?" Things will subside for a few days, only to start up again. I would like for the spirits to leave me alone. I have no idea why they enjoy bothering me this way. They seem to be at their most annoying during the day, because everything that I have told to you has happened to me only in the day hours.

One day, as I was vacuuming the third–floor hallway, a shad-

"I refused to go into that room without someone else being with me."

owy figure came right up to me and brushed against my left side. The shadow was moving quickly, and I got the impression it was of a man. It also seemed to be threatened and angry, because of the manner in which it pushed me. I was so scared that I dropped what I was doing and dashed out of the room. Because I needed to finish cleaning that room, I located a fellow employee and asked her to accompany me. I refused to go into that room without someone else being with me.

A friend of mine who used to work at the hotel once told me that she had seen the ghost of an old lady. That ghost appeared twice to my friend. There is also a male employee who works the front desk who on several occasions, has seen the ghost of an old woman. He told me that the ghost appears on the stairwell by the elevator, dressed in a white dress.

I also recall an employee who worked for the hotel for just a day. She was hired as a maid, and while she was cleaning a room, she was actually attacked by a ghost! She told me that the ghost grabbed hold of her body and would not let her go! She struggled and struggled, but it held on. The supervisor soon called an ambulance that took her to the hospital. After that experience, she never returned to work.

I do not want to see a ghost ever! I try to be firm with the ghosts when they start to play tricks on me. I keep telling them to understand that I have to work for a living, that I don't want to be scared. I really don't like to be alone in empty rooms, but what can I do? It's my job I don't have much choice, do I?

History of The Jerome Grille and Inn building

The Clinkscale building was constructed in 1899 and has been in continuous operation since that time. It originally housed a hardware store on the first floor and offices on the second. Its history is as varied and colorful as the town of Jerome itself.

The building is made of poured re-enforced concrete, with walls up to 18 inches thick. The original owners wanted the building to be as fireproof as possible, because it had been on the ashes of the third major fire that had devastated the town within the previous 18 months. As documented in the Jerome Reporter Supplement of December 28, 1899, this build-

ing was the creation of J.G. Clinkscale, a California and Arizona insurance ad-juster, as an "ornament to the City."

The Inn at Jerome is an elegantly restored Victorian inn that boast eight guest rooms, including one named, "Spooks, Ghosts and Goblins." The proprietors have given great care to detail and have selected all the furnishings with comfort in mind. Genuine goose down pillows compliment each bed, as does memorabilia of the West. A large parlor and fireplace is always available to guests for quiet conversation (perhaps a ghost story or two), and incredible views of the Verde Valley may be seen from the many windows which provide vistas of Sedona's Red Rock County and the mountains of Flagstaff's San Francisco Peaks.

Billie Jo Shepherd's Story

Billie Jo Shepherd

I've been working at the Grille as head waitress for about a year, but I've also worked upstairs in the Inn. In fact, the Inn is where I first saw what I would call a ghost. Of course, I was told about the place being haunted, but those stories don't mean much until a person experiences such things first-hand. When my friends found out that I got the job at the Inn, the first thing I was told was, "Be careful! Don't you bring back any ghosts with you!"

I had been working only two months when I experienced a ghost. It was about 4 pm, and I was in the room named "Victorian Rose." Now, this might sound a bit unusual, but I saw a shadow of a man move across the room and then go behind the door! Yes, I was scared, so scared that I ran down the stairs to the first floor! I'm not a superstitious person, but this did frighten me.

Today, I'm working downstairs in the Grille restaurant, but I guess the ghost doesn't care where I work because just last week I had something else happen to me. I was alone in the early morning when I thought I heard the cook walk in. I heard footsteps approach me from behind. I began to speak out loud, thinking that I was talking to the cook. When there was no verbal response, I turned around and there was that same dark figure of a man I saw upstairs, standing with his head bent to one side. He just stood there looking at me with a cold stare. I let out a loud scream, and then that thing disappeared!

About five minutes later, the cook came in. I told him about what I had just seen, and he paid close attention to my story.

After I finished, he told me about his own experiences with a ghost that rubs against him. You might want to speak to him and get his story. He said that it rubs against him like a large cat would do. Isn't that strangest thing you ever heard?

JoAnne Chasteen's Story

JoAnne Chasteen

I've been working at the inn for close to three years as the housekeeper, and I'm originally from Southern California. As soon as I told local friends about my new job, they congratulated me, and then they shared their stories about the building being haunted.

I had my own ghostly encounter one day while I was cleaning a room named "Lariat and Lace." I keep feeling uncomfortable as I worked, as if someone was in the room with me, watching every move I made. I couldn't seem to shake this feeling. Then I saw the movement of people's shadows in the room. These shadows moved away from me, and then disappeared!

There have been several other times when I was in a room getting it clean for the next guests' arrival. I do the usual routine things like dusting and making the bed with fresh sheets and pillow cases. After having made a bed, I returned just a few minutes later and would be surprised to see the impression on the comforter and pillow, of a person's body! I have no idea how this could happen. Not wanting to leave the bed in such a condition, I would once again fluff the pillow and straighten out the wrinkles on the bed. I knew that a ghost must have been responsible or playing a game with me. As I turned away for a second or two, the pillow once more would have the same impression! This weird thing has happened to me in two particular rooms "Kiss and Tell" and "Pillow Talk." I don't necessarily feel frightened when this happens, just annoyed.

I also know that the inn has cold and hot spots; areas where extreme temperature changes are felt for no reason. The staff knows about these things, especially the ones that have been with the inn for several years. I have heard of strange things happening in the kitchen, such as trays of glasses and dishes being thrown to the floor and broken. In the area of the bar, bottles of liquor have also been knocked to the floor and broken.

All in all, I don't think I would like to experience such things any more. I enjoy a quiet and peaceful workplace. I know that upstairs in the inn, things are peaceful, but downstairs in the Grille, well... that's another story.

KINGMAN

Kingman is located in northwestern Arizona at the intersection of Interstate 40 and U.S. 93. Kingman is situated in the Hualapai Valley between the Cerbat and Hualapai Mountain Ranges at an elevation of 3,400 feet. The city was established in the early 1880s by Lewis Kingman who located the route of the Santa Fe Railway. It was incorporated in 1952 and has served as county seat of Mohave County since 1887.

Kingman is a regional trade, service, and distribution center for northwestern Arizona. Its strategic location relative to Los Angeles, Las Vegas, Phoenix, Laughlin and the Grand Canyon has made tourism, manufacturing/distribution, and transportation –leading industries.

My interview with the Greers was held in their kitchen while we shared a pizza. The Greers are a wonderful retired couple who have enjoyed living in Kingman since their move from California. Charlie raises gourds in his large back yard, while Ursula paints and decorates them with fancy designs. Their house is filled with these crafts. Several times a year, the Greers box up their decorated gourds, and in their RV, they tour the states, selling them at flea markets and craft fairs.

The Greers' personal ghost story is equally unique and curiously unusual as the Greers themselves.

Ursula and Charlie Greer's Story

We've only lived in Kingman for two years. Originally we both are from Los Angeles, California and decided to leave Los Angeles because of the problems with crime, smog, and everything else that goes along with living in a big city. Generally, we just got tired of the rat race.

We looked all over the state of Arizona and decided on relocating to Kingman because of its location, right on Interstate 40. Yeah, we'd heard all the jokes about how hot the summers can be from our friends back in California. It does get very hot out here, but just like everyone else in Kingman, we've gotten used to scheduling our outdoor activities to start before the sun rises and after it sets. It's not so bad.

The house we bought was built in 1952, so that makes it 44 years old this year. That's not too old as far as houses go, but old enough for it to be haunted! I guess this is a good place to begin our story about what's been going on here since we moved in.

Charlie and I were only in the house for the first night when we heard what sounded like a heavy branch of a tree being blown by the wind against the side of the house, a scratching sound. We were both asleep, and this noise was loud enough to wake us both up. Charlie got out of bed and took a peek out the bedroom window. He was expecting to see a strong wind blowing sand and trash all about the yard, but it was as still as could be. I thought that perhaps a stray dog or cat had been the cause of the noise, but we didn't see any animals. Soon the noise stopped, and we thought nothing further about it and went right back to sleep.

Well, this did not happen again for a couple of weeks, until one night when I was busy in the living room unpacking a large cardboard box from our move. Charlie had driven into town and was visiting with a friend. Since I was alone in the house, I turned on the radio and tuned it to a country station. A song came on I liked, so I turned up the volume. After turning away from the radio, I took a passing glance at the direction of the kitchen, when I saw who I thought was my husband, Charlie, walk past the doorway. Over the sound of the radio I yelled at Charlie, "Hey, boy, what are you doing back so soon? You trying to scared me sneaking in like that! " Normally Charlie would respond, but this time there was no response. I walked to the kitchen, and there on the table was a man's hat. I stopped in my tracks and again I called out for Charlie. When there was no reply, I went to the door that led out to the back yard. It was locked from the inside!

I turned around to look at the hat. It was a dirty brown

"There on the table was a man's hat!"

color, covered with dust, with a wide, old, satin band stained by perspiration. I noticed it had a strong smell of wet earth. I placed it back down on the table, and I immediately got a frightening chill that took over my body. I dashed for the front door yelling, "Charlie, Charlie, where are you?" As I got outside, I went around the back of the house and saw nothing unusual. I decided that I did not want to be in the house alone, so I waited out in the street until I spotted Charlie's car driving towards me in the darkness, about an hour later.

I guess Charlie can explain how I reacted from this point.

Charlie's Explanation:

When I drove up to the house, I was surprised to see Ursula standing in the middle of the street. I parked the car in the driveway, and she came right up to me before I even opened the car door. I got out, and she grabbed me and began to cry. She told me quickly that there was a stranger in our home who had been watching her and that she had probably scared him away, but she was not sure of it. I opened the trunk of the car and brought out a small steel pipe which I used as an extension handle for a wrench. Armed with this weapon, we entered the house, with me leading the way.

We completely searched each room and found the entire house to be empty. The old hat that Ursula discovered on the kitchen table was nowhere to be found. There was not a trace of anyone in the house other than the two of us.

About a week passed without another incident, but soon Ursula began to have strange dreams. These dreams were very scary even to me. I was awakened by her moaning and screaming. As I turned on the light in our bedroom, I saw that she was covered in sweat. I shook her in order to wake her, she opened her eyes and whimpered. I knew something was not right. When I asked her to tell me her dreams, she did not want to discuss anything until the next morning. She can tell you what she was dreaming about those nights.

Ursula's Explanation:

All I remember is dreaming of this older man—whom I did not recognize—approach me with a very painful look on his face. In my dream he is wearing that very same hat which I found that night on the kitchen table. He would take short steps towards me, as though limping. I guess that is what seems the most frightening to me, his limping. Then he holds out both arms and takes a strong jump towards me! This is when I begin to scream with all my might, and Charlie wakes me.

One thing that Charlie did not mention was that one night when I was having the same bad dream, he woke me and as I lay there in bed, I told Charlie that my shoulder was hurting. When Charlie turned on the light we saw the red marks of a man's fingers left on my shoulder! Boy, were we scared. I told Charlie, "See, that's what I've been afraid of all along, that that man would grab me!"

Soon after, my bad nightmares stopped, but that was not the end of it. One day I decided to speak to the realtor who sold us the house. I was a little apprehensive, but I informed her about what Charlie and I had experienced at the house. The realtor said that I should go to the town of Truxton about 20 north of Kingman and speak with a man who was the seller of our house named J. B. That very afternoon Charlie and I drove to Truxton and met with J. B. The story he told us really made us believers of the existence of ghosts. This is what J. B. told us:

Many years ago, the original owner of our house, Mr. Altenberry was riding his horse in the foothills of the Hualapai mountains just south of Kingman. He and a friend were riding on a trail, and everything was going fine until his friend's horse was spooked by a rattlesnake. The horse reared back and knocked Mr. Altenberry's friend off the horse.

Well, Mr. Al-tenberry decided to teach the rattlesnake a lesson, so he dismounted his horse and approached the snake. The rattler was a big son-of-a-gun, about a six-footer! Mr. Altenberry used a stick he found to coax the snake out of from under a bush, and with his friend's help, they used a large

"He was riding his horse into the Hualapai mountains."

rock to kill the poor animal. Apparently, the two men were so overjoyed with their successful hunting skills that they decided to gather up the limp trophy and take it back into Kingman to display to all who wished to listen to their story.

Mr. Altenberry took hold of the creature's tail and held it up above his head for his partner to determine the serpent's actual length. No sooner had he lifted its tail above his head, the once lifeless head quickly turned around and sunk its fangs into his thigh! Boy, were the men surprised!

With all the commotion that took place, both horses took off at a gallup, and the two men were left to chase after their horses before going back to town for medical attention. A few hours later, one of the horses was caught, while the other was "spooked real good" and refused to be captured. By this time, the ailing Mr. Altenberry's whole leg was swollen. The snake's toxin was doing its job, and he knew he was in a bad situation.

The two men decided that Mr. Altenberry should ride the one remaining horse into town. Mr. Altenberry was in such a terrible state, he began to shake violently. His friend knew that he would not be able to ride alone, so Mr. Altenberry was left at that spot while his friend rode at a gallop into town for help. Apparently, Mr. Altenberry's friend stated that Mr. Altenberry must have been aware of his terminal fate, as he could

"He took hold of the creature's tail and held it up above his head."

hear his friend's screams of pain as he rode into the distance.

Soon a team of men returned and arrived at the spot where Mr. Altenberry had last been seen. They found his body sprawled over a boulder. He knew that someone would return for him, so, with the last bit of strength he could manage, he hung his hat on a top branch of a nearby desert palo verde tree, in the hope that they would spot his hat and locate his body.

Well, that was the story that J. B. told to Charlie and me. We were satisfied with what we now knew and how it related to the

limping man in my dreams, the dusty hat in my kitchen, and the man I had spotted walking in my house. I don't want to experience any more ghost of the "limping ghost" in the house. We have not heard or seen anything else. I sure hope we don't.

NOGALES

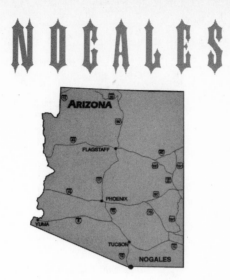

Nogales, Arizona and its twin city, Nogales, Sonora, Mexico are on the international border separating the United States and Mexico. The Arizona city serves as both the economic capital and the county seat of Santa Cruz County, the smallest and southernmost of Arizona's counties. The city is in a mountainous setting, at an elevation of 3,865 feet. Nogales was established in 1880 by Jacob and Isaac Isaacson, who built a trading post along the border. Two years later, Nogales was the site of the first rail connection between Mexico and the United States. Nogales incorporated in 1893.

International commerce is an important part of the Nogales economy. Its location makes Nogales a vital retail hub for shoppers from Northern Mexico. More than 40 percent of Nogales' sales tax comes from the 50,000 Mexican shoppers crossing the border on an average day.

Nogales, Arizona and sister city Nogales, Sonora, Mexico, are home to one of the largest cooperative manufacturing (maqiladora) clusters along the U.S.-Mexico border. The maquiladora concept uses U.S. manufacturing plants located on both sides of the border to take advantage of favorable wage and operating costs and excellent transportation and distribution networks.

Dorotea Rios's Story

I interviewed Dorotea at her home one early morning. Dorotea was not shy about revealing her age of 74 years. Although she has had a plentiful life thus far, there have been a few tragedies to overcome. One in particular was the death of her husband many years ago. Her husband died in a mining accident and left her with a baby son to raise. Her son also lives nearby.

Dorotea surrounds her three-bedroom house with a lovingly-tended garden of hollyhocks and sunflowers and her favorite: pink rose bushes. Proudly displayed in her home are photos of her husband, son, and grandchildren.

At times during the interview, Dorotea's small cage of parakeets located in the kitchen would commence to wildly chirping and tweeting. In a sweet, calm voice Dorotea would say to me in Spanish, "I hope they don't bother you too much, but you know they are my little friends. God has given us those little animals so that we can always have music in life."

Dorotea is a beautiful and sincere woman who spends her days tending to her birds and garden. On her kitchen window sill, she keeps a small old picture of a strange man, and next to it, a small vase with a single flower. The story of Dorotea's simple gesture to this strange fellow in the picture now follows.

One evening seven years ago, I was alone in my bedroom when I heard a noise coming from the living room. I got up off my chair and walked into the dark hallway. I turned on the light and noticed a large figure of a man standing by the front door. I was scared because I didn't recognize this man. I asked him, "Who are you? What do you want?" He did not answer me, so I said, "Please leave my house, please leave my house." Again he did not answer me. I stood there amazed that a stranger had somehow gotten into my house.

The ghost was wearing dark-colored trousers, suspenders, and a white shirt, and his hair was combed back. I also noticed that he had big ears! I began to get really frightened, and I guess he sensed this because he took some steps away from me. I let out a scream and that's when he disappeared!

Immediately I knew this was a ghost, and it left me shaking. I was so scared that night that I couldn't even think of sleeping. I decided to turn on the radio and leave all the lights on. I put on my coat and walked over to my neighbors,' who lived a short walk away from me. I needed to get away from my house, I was so scared. I told my friend about what I had seen, and she could see how frightened I was because I began to cry. I spent the night at her house, and in the morning she accompanied me to my house. As we entered my house—aside from the lights and radio being on—there was nothing out of place.

I had never experienced anything like this before. I began to think that I had imagined the ghost. I thought "was I going crazy?" I could not get the image of the ghost out of my mind. I guess I wanted to know who this ghost was. Was he a relative of mine, a friend, or what?

After that night, I did not experience the ghost for about a year. Then one early morning at dawn, I was awakened by the sound of my birds making loud noises in the kitchen. As I entered the kitchen, I saw the ghost once again. This time he was seated at the table. He just stared at me with big, dark eyes. Because the kitchen windows faced east, the morning light coming through the curtains lit the room just enough for me to make out the details of his face. I got the courage to ask him to tell me who he was. He kept quiet and then slowly turned his head to one side. I saw that he had a large wet area just above his right ear. I was standing about ten feet away, and as I stared, I noticed that he had an injury. I began to feel a weakness overcome my body. I held onto the door jam and pleaded to the ghost to leave my home.

I didn't notice when the ghost disappeared, because it happened so quickly. I phoned my neighbor, who came right over to my house. We discussed the situation, and she decided it would be best to contact a priest. I was so scared about angering the ghost that I decided not to have a priest come to the house. I didn't want to risk having this ghost return to do something to me. I just didn't want to stir things up anymore.

My neighbor mentioned my problem to her sister who worked at the local senior center. Soon after, I received a call from a woman at the center who said that she too had heard

"She asked me if this was the ghost I had seen in my house."

my story and had information which I might wish to hear. I told her that I would like to visit with her, to discuss what she knew. She agreed to meet that evening at her home.

I informed my neighbor about my conversation with the woman and our meeting. I also asked if she and her sister could accompany me to this meeting. She agreed and that night my neighbor drove the three of us to the woman's home.

The woman was surprised to see all of us, but was nonetheless, very welcoming. After I told her my story, she explained why she thought I was being visited by the ghost. The ghost, she said, was that of a man who was a close friend of her family's. The young man's name was Edward Buckwith and he spoke fluent Spanish. He lived in Tucson and visited her family every time he passed through Nogales on his return trip from Mexico. He had a contact in Mexico who supplied him with liquor. At the time, Prohibition was in full swing, and it was illegal to bring liquor into the United States. Lots of men were involved in this illegal business, but it was not a safe profession.

The woman continued her story. "One evening, after having dinner at our house, Edward left our home. My parents were unaware of what happened next until the following day. Apparently, he was surrounded by some hooligans who knew he was carrying liquor, and they beat him up. One of the men kicked Edward in the head so hard, he passed out. After beating him, they rolled his body down the small ravine that used to be located next to the house. He landed face down in a small amount of water, which caused him to drown," she said.

The woman further said that she believed the ghost I had seen was Edward's because of my description of his large ears. Then she brought out a picture and asked me if this was the ghost I had seen in my house. I was shocked! The ghost I had seen twice in my house was now staring back at me from the picture I was holding in my hand!

The woman said, "As soon as I heard about the ears, I knew it had to be Edward." She further said, "Why Edward had chosen to appear to your house is a mystery to me." She said this because my house is not the house that her family used to live in. Her house was directly next door to my house. I didn't know how to respond, except to say that all this was making me a nervous wreck. I asked her what I could do to end his visits. She answered, "Take the picture and place it in your house and

ask Eddie to go on to heaven. Tell him you know he was murdered and that you feel sorry about this, but you can't do anything else for him."

I returned home with the picture and placed on the kitchen
counter with a flower. I prayed and said the words the woman
had told me to say. After a few weeks, I revisited the woman to
return the picture. She asked me to keep and display it the way
I had been doing. "What good would it do me now? He chose
your house, not mine."

PARKER

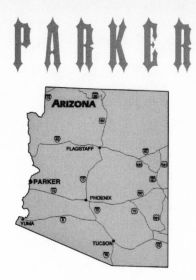

Parker is on the east bank of the Colorado River, 163 miles west of Phoenix. The Parker "vicinity" consists of a number of separate but interrelated areas: Parker, Parker South, the Arizona side of the Colorado river area, and the communities on the California side. Established in 1871, the town was later moved some four miles north to the site of the Atchison, Topeka and Santa Fe Railroad crossing. At an elevation of 450 feet above sea level, Parker was founded in 1908 and incorporated in 1948. In May 1982, by initiative petition voters formed La Paz County from the northern portion of the former Yuma County. On January 1, 1983, Parker became the county seat for La Paz county.

Parker's economy is based primarily on retail trade and services. The 16-mile strip of the Colorado River, between Parker Dam and Headgate Rock Dam, forms one of the finest bodies of water in the country for water-based recreational activities.

This makes Parker a major destination point for tourists and winter visitors.

Brian Doran's Story

My interview with Brian took place at his sister-in-law's home. Brian is an 87 year-old native-born Irishman. Born in 1910 in county Wicklow, Brian, his parents, and his two sisters arrived in the United States when he was only seven years of age. The Doran family lived in Philadelphia for ten years, after which Brian decided to make the solo move west. His traveling eventually led him to the town of Tucson, where he worked as a construction worker. In 1968 he moved to Parker and found a job as a plumber. In 1969 he met and married Becky, a local woman originally from Colorado. The following year he and his new wife had a baby girl, whom they named Kenna. Kenna survived until age 3. On the baby's death certificate, "trauma to the head due to a fall," is listed as the cause of death.

Becky discovered little Kenna's lifeless body on the kitchen floor one afternoon. Kenna had apparently run into the table with her head and knocked herself unconscious. Becky was hanging the wet laundry in the backyard and did not notice what had happened. She went to check on her baby whom she had laid on the living room sofa for a noontime nap just an hour or so before.

After the death of their daughter, the Dorans did not have anymore children. In 1975 Becky herself was involved in a car accident on Interstate 10 and died.

There's no doubt that Brian has suffered many deep heartaches in his life. Given his trials, he remains focused on celebrating life and stated to me his personal dictum of life; "God put us here on earth to be judged, not to judge."

There remains much to be told of Brian's life; What follows is only one segment of that fascinating and at times difficult unwritten biography of this special man.

The death of my little girl left both my wife and me with an empty hole in our lives. We had been so happy, Kenna brought us so much joy and pride. My wife and I were never fully convinced about what caused our baby's death. How could a fall have caused a 3-year-old's death? The doctor who examined Kenna's body told us that because she hit her head with such force, it caused a bruise or blood clot to form on her brain. This blood clot affected her lungs, and she stopped breathing. Without oxygen reaching her brain, the brain became damaged, and she died.

With the death of our little Kenna, our dreams ended. Soon my wife's personality changed. Becky no longer laughed. We began to argue, our marriage was in trouble. We were filled with depression and sadness. Not long after, my wife was taken away from me in a car accident.

So now I was left totally alone in an empty house. I was such an emotional mess during that time. I was fortunate to have the members of my church, who helped me through the tough times. They also helped with Becky's funeral arrangements. When the time came to pack and donate my wife's clothes my daughter's toys and things—well, if not for their help, I don't know what I would have done. It was just a few weeks later, that I was visited by my baby's spirit.

I was sitting in the living room one evening listening to a radio talk show. It was about 9:30 pm. All the lights in the house were out except for the light over the stove and a lamp on my living room table. Suddenly, I heard the sound of a coughing child. I turned to look in the direction of the kitchen and I saw, standing in the doorway, my little girl! I was so shocked to see her that I could not move. Instead of immediately saying something, I began to sob like a baby!

It took me a few seconds, but soon I called out her name. I felt her unblinking eyes stare deep into my soul. "Kenna, my little Kenna," I cried, "I've missed you so much!" She responded to my plea by raising her arms and placing her hands to her throat. This gesture told me something was wrong. Quietly, and with much pain on her little face, she began to cough and rub her throat once again. Try as I might, I could not get up off the chair. It was as if I were glued firmly in place!

I cried out, "Baby, what is wrong with your throat?" Again she rubbed her neck and made sounds of painful suffering. I said, "What is wrong with your throat? What is it?"

Then she cried out, "Daddy, Daddy!" At that point I was overtaken by a deep feeling of despair and helplessness. I broke down into an uncontrollable, shaking and crying mess. I wanted to help and go to my child, but I could not move out of the chair! I sobbed and sobbed and when I looked up at her, she again said, "Daddy!"

I answered, "Yes, yes, baby, I know you hurt! I promise I will help you!" Then she slowly disappeared! I soon regained the ability to lift myself out of the chair, went to my bedroom and cried myself to sleep. I knew that Kenna had appeared to me for a reason. The following day an answer to came to me.

The next morning, I was in the backyard mending a wire fence. Strangely, I heard a voice in my head, something like a mental message, telling me to contact the local cemetery office. I had always had doubts about my daughter's cause of death. I was never fully satisfied with the doctor's summary.

Now the apparition of my daughter the night before this only caused me to wonder even more. I needed to know once and for all how she died. If it would take another autopsy, well, so be it! I could not erase the image of Kenna's little spirit coughing and rubbing her throat from my mind.

I contacted the cemetery office and also spoke to our local marshall about the possibility of an autopsy. I was met with strange looks, but overall, everything went smoothly. They informed me that there was no reason why I could not go through with my desire, but I would have to contact a medical examiner in Phoenix, to do the actual autopsy. Of course, I did not tell the marshall about my daughter's ghostly visit, or anything which would give anyone cause to view me as a crazy old man. It took a few weeks to get the necessary paperwork, and within a couple of months, everything was in place.

The total cost for an autopsy was unbelievably expensive, but I was determined. The memory of Kenna standing in the kitchen doorway with such a painful expression on her face gave me the strength I needed to push ahead. Finally, the day of the disinterment took place, and my little girl's body and coffin were taken to a medical lab in Phoenix.

Tissue, hair, and blood samples were taken, as were X-rays. After 20 days, I received a phone call from the lab and was asked to drive to Phoenix. The attending doctor wanted to speak with me in person. I arrived at the lab and was escorted into a room with a light box on the wall, used for viewing X-rays. Soon the doctor and a medical assistant—carrying an oversize envelope of X-rays entered the room.

The doctor informed me of the tests results. She stated that all the tests showed Kenna to be in normal health at the time of her death. I was relieved to hear this, but before I could feel content with this updated information, the doctor switched on the light box and removed from the envelope the x-rays taken of Kenna's small head and neck. Immediately, I knew that something was not right. On the X-rays was a small object that showed up as a bright white little square in Kenna's throat!

The doctor told me that when she viewed the X-rays, it was clear that this unusual square object needed to be investigated. When the foreign object was removed from Kenna's little throat, the doctor discovered that it was a sewing thimble! The doctor estimated that Kenna must have swallowed the thimble, and it had lodged in her throat, causing her to choke. In a panic, Kenna must have run throughout the house, reached the kitchen, lost consciousness, fainted, and hit her head. The trauma to her head was obvious because of the skin bruising and the large swollen area where she hit the table. This visible sign of injury was enough for the initial examiner to conclude his reason for her cause of death.

I was both greatly surprised and immediately satisfied with the results of this second autopsy. A feeling of satisfaction came over me. No longer did I have any doubts; no longer did the cause of my one and only child's death haunt me. Finally the spirit of my baby girl would be at peace.

On the return drive home to Parker from Phoenix, I could only imagine what my wife's reaction might have been if she were still alive. I believe that Kenna's ghostly visitation was for a purpose. She wanted me to be at peace, to know that her daddy would also find peace from his loneliness. No one can ever tell me that there is no life after death. I have seen my baby, and I know better!

PHOENIX

Phoenix, known as the Valley of the Sun, is the seventh largest city in the nation. The city is the hub of the rapidly growing Southwest and the heart of a metro area of 245 million. Phoenix also is the capital of Arizona and the Maricopa County seat. In 1867, Phoenix founder Jack Swilling formed a canal company and diverted irrigation water from the Salt River. Soon many farms were operating, but drought periods hampered production. In 1911, Roosevelt Dam was completed and water supplies were stabilized. Cotton and citrus became the most important crops.

Phoenix's explosive growth began during World War II when military airfields were built in Maricopa County for the near-perfect flying weather. Many defense industries followed. Luke Air Force Base, west of Phoenix, is still a major training center for fighter pilots.

The Phoenix climate has been a major factor in its economic development: the area experiences sunshine nearly every day of the year.

The name Phoenix - legendary Egyptian symbol of rebirth - was chosen because the city was built on the ruins of the Hohokam Indian civilization, whose farmers laid out irrigation canals still in use today.

Phoenix has a diversified economic base. Manufacturing is a leading employer with 148,000 people working for 3,100 firms in the metro area. Electronics is a strong component. The area currently ranks third among electronic production centers in the country. Tourism is an important income producer. Many world-class hotels and resorts cater to visitors.

Yolanda Huerta's Story

I interviewed Yolanda at her home on the far north side of the city. Yolanda has lived in Phoenix for 14 years. Born and raised in Phoenix, she moved to Los Angeles to attend college and eventually marry. Her marriage was in her own words, "a disaster." After her divorce, single and without children, this 42-year-old woman decided to return to the city of her birth. She bought a small lot of land on the north side of the city, and purchased a two-bedroom mobile home.

Due to the extreme heat Phoenix is famous for, Yolanda built a ramada (arbor) directly outside her front door, and under which our interview was conducted. While sitting under its protective wood slats, the ramada offered us much welcomed shade from the intense heat of the day. Looking out from the ramada to the north is a dramatic, panoramic view of the Tonto national forest. This forest is composed of a blanket of desert flora, including saguaro cactus, palo verde (green thin-trunked trees), prickly pear, and other such drought tolerant plants. The mountains rise in their unique and contorted splendor up to the blue sky. What a sight! "I love it here," Yolanda said, "I have several coyotes come visit me each night. They sniff around and catch any mice that might want to make a dash inside my home."

Looking to the east, my eyes caught the sight of several large homes, and further beyond, even more indications of human encroachment upon the desert landscape. "Things sure have changed

120

here since I was a child," Yolanda said "My whole family used to hike in the foothills each summer and gather saguaro tunas (fruit). Mom would make a jam out of the tunas. It was delicious! Now with all the changes and rapid growth of this city, it's hard for me to even comprehend how things used to be back then."

I had a wonderful time listening to Yolanda's stories about the times she spent up in the mountains. I especially enjoyed the story she told me about the time she and a girlfriend hiked into the Tontos one spring and experienced something unforgettable—something frighteningly unforgettable.

Last year my friend Erlinda and I were sitting right out here one evening, under this ramada. We were enjoying a few beers and talking about how frustrated we both were about how life was going for us. We decided that the best thing for us to do would be to get away from "the world" and hike for a couple of days and nights into the mountains. We had done this before, so we were well prepared for the journey. Our sleeping bags and backpacks were dusted off, and within two days we were off!

The first day of our journey was wonderful. We had brought along plenty of water and food so we knew we would get along fine. On our second day, we decided to change our usual course, which was to follow the trail north, veering to the east, hoping to go around a large mountain and meet up with the trail up ahead. We hiked for hours, until the sun began to cast long shadows on the ground. Earlier in the day, we had decided to make camp for the night while the sun was still out. We spotted a blue tent just off the trail about a mile ahead. As we got closer, we heard beautiful music. A small dog barked at us as we approached the tent, and a young guy who was playing a flute turned and waved hello to us. We stopped and talked to this interesting guy. He was from Taos, New Mexico. After a while, we were introduced to his wife, who we had awakened from her nap in the tent. They invited us to pitch our tent next to theirs for the night. Erlinda and I agreed that it would be a good idea, so we chose a patch of ground with the least amount of rocks and pitched our tent.

We had an interesting conversation with our new friends about city life versus living with just the basics as we passed around a bag of trail mix. Even though the sun was just setting in the west, there was still plenty of light. Suddenly, their dog began to growl at something in the distance. We stopped our conversation to look in the direction of the dog. We were surprised to see a figure of a woman running over the landscape, about a 200 feet from us. She was a short woman and had shoulder length hair. Surprisingly, she was naked and holding on to her stomach! We were definitely caught off guard by the woman. I yelled at her, and she must have heard me, because she stopped running and turned to faced us. We could see that she was not acting in a normal manner. Again I yelled, and she just stood there, frozen in place. Erlinda said she was going to walk over to the woman. I decided to go as well.

"She ran into a small grove of palo verdes."

As we came about 40 or 50 feet from her, she turned away and ran into a small grove of palo verdes. We got close enough to her to see her facial features. The woman was an American Indian. What instantly alarmed us was the *blood* that covered her hands and stomach! I yelled at her not to run away, as both Erlinda and I attempted to catch up to her. When we got to the palo verdes, there was no trace of her. She had disappeared! There was no way anyone could have gotten away from us that quickly. The whole episode left us disturbed. The poor woman's face was filled with so much fear and panic. It was difficult to get that picture out of my mind. Just then, the couple we were camping with came up to us.

The wife asked us where the woman went. We had no answer. They must have seen the look of amazement on our faces because they lowered their voices and said, "Are you all right? What happened, what did you see?" I began to shake with fear as I answered, "We've just seen a ghost!" Erlinda said, "Let's get the hell out of here, *now!*" Once back at the camp we told them the details of the woman and her bloody stomach.

The couple decided, while there was still enough light, to return to the grove of palo verdes and search for the woman. They looked everywhere in the general area. The couple's dog sniffed the ground but did not seem to pick up any scent. After a while searching, they decided to stop since it was getting dark, and they didn't want to risk the chance of getting bitten by a rattlesnake.

That night it took Erlinda and me a very long time before we felt comfortable enough to fall asleep. The couple who also saw the woman from a distance must have had many more questions they wanted to ask us, but under the circumstances they must have sensed that it would be best to save their questions for the morning.

Morning finally did arrive–not soon enough for Erlinda and me. We discussed the details of the night before and returned to the site of the woman's disappearance. Once again, we did not find a clue or any indication of what had transpired the evening before. Erlinda turned to me and said, "I think it would be best if we hiked back home today, how about you?"

I didn't need any further prodding. I answered, "Let's get going!" We said our good-byes to the couple from Taos and headed on the trail back home.

As you can imagine, all Erlinda and I talked about was the woman. We tried to make sense of what we had seen but, it only caused us to have more questions about something that seemed impossible to explain.

Once at home, I bought and read our local newspapers for any indication of a lost or disappeared woman. I didn't find a thing. The local television news didn't report any missing woman either. Erlinda and I decided to drop the subject and get on with our lives. However, my curiosity prompted me to pick up the phone and give my uncle a call. My uncle is retired after working 25 years for the forest service as a surveyor. I decided to give him a call simply to inquire about anything unusual that he may have experienced or heard of during his employment. He found my questions to be rather odd, but soon told me about several fellow workers who had encountered a woman's ghost that fit my description.

He told me that about 10 years ago, two men were surveying a small track of land further north of the area where Erlinda and I had seen the ghost. He said that the men saw this strange Indian woman running naked among some short desert brush. Aside from her nakedness, the men were interested in another odd occurrence. Getting a better view with binoculars, they could see her disappear and reappear! All this took place in broad daylight.

The woman appeared sporadically and watched the men at their work for the full four days that they were in the area. She never got any closer that several hundred yards from where they were. It was obvious to them that she did not want any-one approaching her. Not wanting to arouse any jokes from their fellow workers back at the office, the two men kept the ghost woman a secret from the other employees. My uncle was the only friend whom they felt secure enough to trust with their information. Aside from what my uncle knew from hearsay information, he was unaware of anyone else experiencing any strange apparitions of this ghostly Indian woman.

Erlinda and I have not heard any more about this ghost. I would like to know what she is doing up there in the desert among the cactus and boulders. Does she have something to tell us about how she died? Who killed her perhaps? Maybe she has appeared to someone else. Whatever the story, I won't be hiking into that part of the mountains ever again.

TOMBSTONE

Tombstone, In Cochise County, is probably the most famous and most glamorized mining town in America. Prospector Ed Schieffeling was told he would only find his tombstone in the "Apache-infested" San Pedro Valley. Thus he named his first silver claim Tombstone, and it became the name of the town.

On a mesa between the Dragoon and Huachuca Mountains at an elevation of 4,540 feet, Tombstone incorporated in 1881.

While the area later became notorious for saloons, gambling houses, and the Earp-Clanton shoot-out, in the 1880s Tombstone was larger than Tucson and had become the most cultivated city in the West. Mas-

sive underground water in the mines and falling silver prices ended the boom in 1886. Having survived the Great Depression and removal of the County Seat to Bisbee, Tombstone in the 1930s became known as the "Town Too Tough To Die."

126

Tombstone's economy has changed drastically since its days as a mining town. The town's colorful history is the key factor for steady growth. In 1962, the Department of the Interior designated Tombstone a Registered Historical Landmark. A restoration zone was established and a commission organized for the preservation of its landmarks. Tourists flock to the town by the thousands, and their business is a mainstay of the economy.

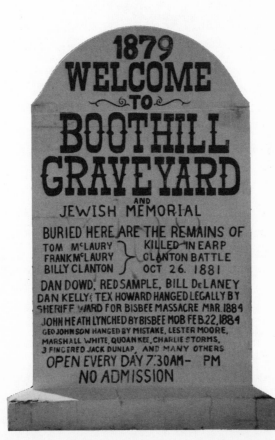

Debbi K. Valdez, Theresa Rice, Tim and Marcy Ferrick

Big Nose Kate's Saloon

In the 1800's, "Big Nose Kate's Saloon" was once The Grand Hotel. Although the saloon itself was not in existence during Tombstone's flourish, it has on its own made quite a mark on Tombstone. The saloon is named after the woman who had quite a rambunctious relationship with John Henry "Doc" Holliday. Doc, a former dentist and a well known gambler in town, never married Kate, although she remained his live-in girlfriend for many years. This great hotel hosted such infamous personalities as Wyatt and Virgil Earp, Holliday, the Clantons, and the McLaurys.

The bar of the present saloon is located on the first floor, but originally, when it was The Grand Hotel, the bar was located downstairs in the basement. The present bar is the only original Tombstone bar which is still in use to this very day.

The Legend of "The Swamper"

During the The Grand Hotel's golden era, a man known as "The Swamper" who worked as a janitor also did odd jobs for the hotel in exchange for his room and board. He was a trusted

and honest hotel aid. The Swamper had his own special bedroom, was located in the dark basement of the hotel, which he
used as his own private haven. He enjoyed the peace and soli-
tude where, separated from the hustle and bustle of the hotel's
many guests above, he could keep his secret of his silvery
wealth to himself.

Throughout the years The Swamper had hoarded and con-
cealed a small fortune of silver somewhere on the premises of
The Grand Hotel. The basement where he lived was deep
enough below the surface of the ground to afford entrance into
one of the catacombing mine shafts that ran underground,
beneath the hotel as well as most of Tombstone. The Swamper
spent many painstaking hours over a period of years tunneling
an entrance into this silver mine shaft. Completing his task, he
gained access to a thick vein of silver where he secretly
extracted, ounce by ounce, glorious silver nuggets.

To this day it is unknown whether The Swamper spent his
silver before his death or hoarded it in an unknown niche
somewhere on the premises of the hotel. Employees of Big
Nose Kate's Saloon however, swear that they have seen The
Swamper's ghost wandering the halls and stairs. Photographers
have caught the ghostly image of an unknown being on a
photo as well as on the postcard of the saloon's interior. Perhaps
the The Swamper, in his afterlife, is protecting the silver still
be buried somewhere in this legendary building.

*I interviewed the following employees of the present Big Nose
Kate's Saloon on a very hot midday in July. I was thoroughly
amazed by everyone's serene composure and easygoing manner as
they described their stories.*

*At one point during the interviews, I was led down a narrow
wooden staircase to the basement of the saloon where the owner, Mr.
Steve Goldstein, pointed out the actual silver mine shaft from which
many stories evolved, including the one of The Swamper. For*

safety's sake, the mine shaft can now be seen through bars of iron. Arranged around the shaft's opening is a collection of antique period furniture of the 1800s. This strange accumulation of dusty furniture, picks, shovels, mirrors, clothing, and oil lamps is made visible only by a few spooky colored light bulbs, which cast an eerie glow on what a miner's life might have looked like.

The stories of the ghosts of Tombstone's violent past will continually resurface. I now present to you just a few of the testimonies by some living individuals who have been witness to weird happenings at Big Nose Kate's Saloon.

Tim L. Ferrick's Story

I am currently the manager of the saloon and have held this position for nine months. I'm originally from Southern California and have visited Arizona and Tombstone repeatedly throughout the last 4 years. During one of my visits to Tombstone, I visited my brother Mick, who at the time was the manager of the saloon. He has since died and is buried at the local cemetery. Before my brother's death, he mentioned to me that he himself had experienced "ghosts" at the saloon. About one month after his funeral, I made plans with my wife to return to Tombstone and meet with the owner of the saloon about taking over my brother's job.

We arrived at Tombstone in the late evening. The owner had closed the doors for the night, and we sat at a table at one corner of the saloon drinking sodas. We discussed a few personal issues, and for some reason, the conversation turned to the strange, ghostly things that employees have experienced at the saloon. Approximately, one half an hour into our discussion, a sudden movement caught all our eyes.

We all turned to look up in the direction of the ceiling of the saloon where a small balcony is located. On the balcony are two mannequins, a man and a woman dressed in 1800's period clothing. We watched as the female mannequin, seated far behind the railing, moved to the railing of the balcony, leaned over, and fell to the floor! As we all sat in our chairs stunned by the noise of the mannequin making contact with the floor, I spotted the male mannequin, who was left facing us. I said to the others at the table, "Hey, take a look at the other mannequin." We all watched as the male mannequin's head quickly turned towards the direction where the female mannequin had been! Truly unnerved by this, we promptly got out of our chairs and called it a night.

The next morning when I spoke to the manager, she stated that since she had no explanation for what had happened. She considered it to be her first ghostly experience at the saloon.

My second experience at the saloon took place about one month after I had begun work. It was about 7:30 am when I began to hear doors opening and closing on their own. I walked to the now opened door—which I had closed and locked just minutes before from the inside—only to see it in an open position! Lights that I personally had turned off were now turned on. During these times, I was the only one in the building!

Returning to my office chair, I suddenly began to hear noises coming from down in the basement where the mine shaft is located. These were the distinctive sounds that a man wearing heavy boots with spurs would make as he walked up or down the stairs. The sound was of someone only walking half way up,or down the stairs, ending in the middle. A few times, after hearing the steps, I rushed to the stairs, hoping to catch a sight of the person making the noise. As soon as I reached the stairs, the footsteps would abruptly stop!

Sometime after these incidents, we decided to install surveillance cameras throughout the saloon. We spent several days installing the cameras in just the right locations, in key rooms of the saloon. The equipment functioned with motion detectors that would sense movement and automatically turn the cameras on to record what ever was present. These sensors were very sensitive to movement, and I was sure we would be able to record any burglar ghost on film. That night before we left the saloon, I personally turned on the motion detectors.

The next morning as I unlocked the back door and entered the building, my wife and I were surprised to see that all the cupboards, doors, refrigerator doors, and drawers were wide open! Nothing had been stolen from the premises. The alarm had not gone on, and I immediately phoned the alarm company to complain that their equipment had failed. The alarm company sent representatives who came over and tested the system and found everything was functioning correctly.

Another experience both my wife and I heard took place one morning. I switched the monitors that were attached to the cameras to scan each room. The camera that was placed in the dance floor of the saloon was picking up a noise. I called my wife over to the TV monitor, and as I turned up the volume, we both clearly heard the sound of booted footsteps walking across the floor! We immediately left the office and entered the dance room where we discovered nothing out of place. A few minutes later, we heard the same footsteps walking in the opposite direction. We knew that something ghostly was happening, but just decided to live with it.

Throughout the years, we have had many patrons experience odd things. Just recently, I was called to witness a gentleman who was in the downstairs bar going through his own supernatural experience. I witnessed as the jacket he was wearing began to press flat against his body! It was as if a large pane of glass was being pressed against him. His wife took a picture of her husband as he was going through the experience, and when she developed it, the large image of a butcher knife appeared floating next to his head! I must admit this incident left me with goose bumps. Other things that have taken place, strangely enough, to just our female employees, have been trash can lids rising off the cans and dropping to the floor, rolling large circular patterns on the floor of the basement. This has happened several times to my own wife. My wife now refers to the ghost as "Felix." It's just a name she decided on, to give the ghost a personality. The male employees have not experienced such things, only the women. We have since removed the trash cans from the basement.

The current owner, Gloria Goldstein, and I heard Gloria's name called out in a very loud, distinctive male voice. We both turned around as she responded, "Yes." There came no response.

Other events patrons have experienced have been the sound of gambling dice being dropped to the floor, sudden cold winds, severe pressure changes in rooms, etc. A lot of these incidents take place randomly. We never gave thought to contacting a priest. We knew we had a ghost and that was it. I know that there is a presence of someone still here in the building. Perhaps a ghost is protecting the place. I'm not afraid, but I do let our employees feel comfortable enough to approach me with their concerns.

Marcy D. Ferrick's Story

My husband Tim and I began employment at the saloon at the same time. I was present in the saloon the evening that Tim spoke about, when we had our first experience; when the mannequins came to life. I gotta say that what we experienced, that night with those mannequins was enough to send us out of there fast!

My second experience with "Felix" happened when I was in the basement. As I entered the basement, suddenly the lid on the trash can popped off and began to roll on the floor. The lid made small circular movements, and then they got bigger and bigger. It just kept moving until I took hold of it and placed it back on the can. Then once more it popped off and repeated the same circular motions on the floor. Again, I took hold of the lid and placed it on the can. Well, this happened for about five times until I had had enough. In a loud and irritated voice I said, "Stop it now!" Then it stopped. I think that "Felix" is trying to harass or tease the women. I don't get the feeling that he is wants to hurt us, just to let us know that he is still here.

Just a couple of months ago, we had two patrons who were very drunk disturbing other patrons with their loud voices. I decided to ask them to leave. When I approached the table, I immediately felt the strong pressure of an invisible male hand on my shoulder. Before I even said a word, the two drunks gazed with very wide eyes in the direction past my shoulder, and immediately put their beers on the table, got up, and made for the door! I then felt the pressure on my shoulder slowly lift up and disappear.

Another strange thing that happens is when I walk down the stairs to the basement. Sometimes I'll notice that the ceiling fan is turning. Thinking that it has been left on, I'll reach for the electrical switch and notice that it is in the "off" position! I'm at a loss to find an explanation for this. We have had the switches checked and have found nothing wrong with the electrical system.

Given all that the other employees and I have experienced in the saloon, I am convinced that it is haunted! I still experience the very distinct footsteps of a heavy-booted and spurred man, who walks up and down the stairs that lead to the basement. I think that the reason "Felix" is so active in the saloon is because he is trapped between the world of the living and of the dead. The first experience I had with the mannequins shocked me and, yes, I was scared, but all the other experiences since have just become a nuisance to me. I'm not scared to be in the building by myself, but you never know what "he" might decide to do next time.

Theresa Rice's Story

I'm originally from Tyler, Texas and have been working at the saloon for seven months as a waitress. My first experience with the ghost of the saloon happen only two weeks after I started work. It was around high noon when I was standing on the south end of the bar.

I was talking to a gentleman customer who was seated across the bar form me. Suddenly, I felt the presence of someone behind me and just as quickly, felt two fingers give my rear end two hard pinches! I immediately turned around to confront the vulgar man who had rudely done this, but when I turned there was no one there! I had been told by other employees that the saloon was haunted. After this experience, I was definitely convinced of this.

My second experience happened just about two months ago. Again, this took place at about noon. I was walking toward the bar, carrying a tray of drinks. Suddenly, I heard a loud male voice call out, "Theresa!" I turned and saw no one. This has happened more than once to me, and also in the presence of others. This initially left me with a confused feeling, but soon I realized that Felix" was behind it. "Felix" is the name the employees have given to what we believe to be "The Swamper." Anyway, I knew Felix was behind everything. I don't know why he chose to play these rude-natured pranks on me. Why is he trying to provoke me? I just wish he would just come out and speak to me. I don't think I would be frightened, but maybe I might be.

Debbie K. Valdez's Story

I'm originally from Whiteland, Indiana, and have been working as a bartender in the second bar that's located downstairs in the basement. I also have a country music band, "Black Velvet," that performs at the saloon. So I'm both a bartender and entertainer. I've been employed at Big Nose Kate's now for seven months. My first experience took place five months after I had begun work at the saloon.

Debbie K. Valdez

It was in the early afternoon when I happened to look up to where the mannequins are located in the balcony. I spotted a very nicely-dressed woman whom I had never seen before. She was dressed in a 1800's period-dark dress, holding a parasol, and her hair was done up in ringlets that were shoulder length. I could not keep my eyes off this strangely beautiful woman. As much as I stared at her, she did not look in my direction, but appeared happy to just observe everyone else down below. Soon I became frightened and felt a coldness come over me. Eventually she disappeared, and I have not seen her since.

Another time, I was wearing my hair pulled back and held in place with a large white bow. Well, apparently the ghost wanted to play with my bow because he kept pulling on it. Several times, I turned my head to see who was tugging at my hair and bow. There was not a living soul. Well, after a few hours of this I got tired of his game and I said, "Now, you stop it!" After that he left me alone.

The ghost also hides my pens. I will write a guest receipt and

136

place the pen on the cash register as I hand the receipt to the customer. I won't even leave the register. As I reach for my pen—*poof*—it's gone! This has happened when more than one person is with me. We look on the floor, behind the register, everywhere! Then in a few minutes, the pen reappears right where I had originally placed it! Now, is that weird or what?

I tend to see lights go on and off in rooms when no one else is with me. I see this quite a lot. I also have seen a gentleman who will sit at the basement bar, wearing a long-sleeved white

"I'm not scared, just a little nervous to be alone down there."

shirt. He just appears quite suddenly, and then just as quickly will disappear. I get the feeling that the ghost does not want to cause me harm, but I have to admit I get very cold chills when I experience these things. The ghost is a playful spirit, and knowing this, I don't like to be left alone in the basement bar. If we have no patrons down below, I'll just walk upstairs to be with someone. I'm not scared, just a little nervous to be alone down there.

TUCSON

Tucson, nicknamed "The Old Pueblo", is Arizona's oldest city, with a unique blend of Native American, Spanish, Mexican, and Anglo heritages. The second largest city in the state, Tucson is modern, with high tech industries and world-class cultural events, yet retains the charm of its desert frontier roots.

Tucson is an Native American word that translates as "water at black mountain." Located beside the Santa Cruz River, it has been home to Native American villages and farms for at least 2,000 years. In 1700, Father Kino established the first Spanish mission, San Xavier, at the Indian village of Bac, 10 miles south of Tucson.

Tucson was founded in 1775 as a Spanish (presidio) or military garrison to protect settlers from Apache raids. It was governed by Mexico from 1821 until 1854, when the Gadsden Purchase made it a part of the United States. Tucson was once the territorial capital of Arizona.

Tucson was incorporated in

138

1877 and is the Pima County seat. At 2,389 feet, it is known for mild winters and very hot summers.

My interview with Florencio was conducted entirely in Spanish, in the same house the Saenz family has owned for over 70 years. Florencio lived in the family's house with his wife of 41 years until her death 12 years ago. They had no children, and today Florencio lives alone in the house with his cat, "Pepino."

Aside from the following story of his uncle, Florencio provided me with numerous details of life as lived in Tucson many years ago. His detailed description of Chicano family life and the various hardships along the way were at times quite touching to hear.

"All us families—the Saenzses, Ortegas, Valenzuelas, Rioses, Barrelas—would gather and have big get-togethers at each other's houses. Those were real nice times. We were all good friends. Some of our children grew up and even married into each other's families. Now, all the old ones from that time are either dead or have moved away."

Today, Florencio spends his days gardening, reading, and attending local church functions. On his bedroom dresser sits a plain old shoe box. Inside is a folded, white cotton cloth containing what remains of four red carnations. "My family has kept these remains for many, many years. I'll always remember the day they arrived in our living room."

Florencio Saenz's Story

I have lived in Tucson all my life. My grandparents were originally from Mesilla, New Mexico, and after they married in the 1920s, they moved to Tucson. We were a very close-knit family, and I was especially close to my father's younger brother, my uncle Julian. As a child, I followed my uncle Julian everywhere. Our family pictures always showed the two of us together. We were inseparable!

Sadly, as my uncle was driving to work one day, he was involved in a serious auto accident. The driver of the other car died at the scene. My uncle was taken to the hospital and placed in the intensive care unit. He was not expected to live for very long.

I took the news very hard, and I remember visiting the hospital with my family and viewing his nearly lifeless body. The awful memories that I can't erase are viewing him in the bed, hooked up to all the tubes, the smell of the room, and the whole atmosphere of the hospital room. It was a terrible time for me. My uncle survived for two weeks in this condition and never regained consciousness.

Late one night, my mother received the phone call that informed us of my uncle's passing. I remember hearing the phone ring and immediately knew that it had to be about my uncle. I was a young boy of 14 years, and his death left a strong impression on me. I refused to eat for several days and would not to speak with anyone. I stayed in my room and even refused to watch my favorite television shows. I became so overcome with sadness that my parents had our local priest come to our home to speak with me. The conversation with the priest did me good, and in a few days, I came out of my depressed state.

My father had a nice picture of my uncle in a drawer with other family pictures. He and my mother decided to frame the picture and display it in our living room. The picture was placed on top of a coffee table together with a small burning candle. It was about a month or so after Uncle Julian was laid to rest that a strange thing began to happen to me.

One evening, as my family and I were gathered in the living room watching television, I turned my head and looked in the direction where my father was seated. There standing directly behind my father was Uncle Julian! I was stunned and unable to speak. I could clearly see my uncle as he looked at me and smiled. He held onto the back of my father's chair. Somehow I knew that I was to keep quiet and not alarm my family. My uncle was speaking to me without moving his mouth. I nervously smiled back and soon the tears began to surface in my eyes. I heard my sister say, "Mom, look at Florencio. He's crying!" As I heard my mother ask me what's wrong, the image of my uncle slowly disappeared.

I got up from my chair and ran to my bedroom. I cried and my mother ran to me. As my mother held me in her arms, I told her what I had just seen. The rest of my family gathered in my bedroom to hear my story. My father put his hands to his face and cried out, "Julian, Julian. God bless you, my brother!"

The second time that my uncle appeared to me took place in the kitchen as we were all having dinner. Again, I saw him standing, but this time he was not behind my father; he stood in the doorway which led from the kitchen to the living room. I didn't cry. This time I just watched in amazement. He gave me a big smile, and I even saw his teeth. I calmly stated to everyone, "My uncle is standing over there; do you see him?" Everyone got quiet and turned in the direction of the doorway. I said, "Look, he's right there!"

"Are you sure?" they responded.

I answered, "Oh, yes, he's right there looking at us." I guess my uncle decided that he had given us enough of a sign because soon his image disappeared.

Throughout the weeks that followed, I saw my uncle appear to me three more times. I decided to keep his appearances to myself, for fear that I might upset my parents. Every time that my uncle appeared, he did not speak to me. His usual posture was to stand at a distance from me and smile. After the the last time he appeared to me, I decided to speak to our family priest about this. I was instructed by the priest to pray and ask my uncle's spirit to go to heaven and be at peace. I did as I was instructed, and I did not see my uncle's spirit for a long time after.

141

One Saturday, my parents decided to take the family to my uncle's graveside and place red carnations—Julian's favorite flowers—at his grave. As I remember, it was a cold but clear day. As we all took turns placing a carnation on the grave, my father broke down with emotion and sobbed. My mother held his hand and tried to console him. Suddenly, I saw the spirit of my uncle appear once again to me. This time there was a difference in his image. He appeared to be more "misty" and he actually spoke!

He said, "Don't be sad. I'm doing very well, and I'm very happy now." As soon as he said these words, his image faded. I told my father what I had just seen and heard.

My father responded, "Florencio, please don't tell me about your dreams anymore. Please, I'm not interested in them!" I knew that I had upset my father and so I kept quiet. We left the cemetery and ate lunch at a local restaurant. My father must have felt that he had hurt my feelings with his words. He told me that sometimes imagination plays tricks on the eyes, and perhaps I should think about what I have been seeing as being something that my imagination conjured up. I knew that what I had seen was my uncle, but not wanting to upset my father any more, I agreed with him and kept quiet.

When we arrived home, a neighbor met us in our front yard and engaged both my parents in conversation. After a few minutes, my mother excused herself and opened the front door to our house and walked inside. She called out to my father who was still speaking with the neighbor to come inside the house. As my father and my sister and I entered the living room, on the coffee table we spotted next to my uncle's picture four red carnations!

My mother was shaking with emotion as she said, "Who put these flowers here?" There were no visitors that the neighbor informed us of. My father picked up the flowers, and as he held them he said, "It doesn't matter. It's a sign from my brother that he is now doing fine." I knew then that my uncle Julian had given my family a sign to convince them of his appearances

I spoke up and said, "Yes, my uncle is going to be fine. I told you he spoke to me. Everything is going to be fine."

And so it has been.

WICKENBURG

Wickenburg is 50 miles northwest of Phoenix at an elevation of 2,100 feet. Nestled in the foothills of the Bradshaw Mountains, and along the banks of the Hassayampa River, Wickenburg boasts a rich Western history, still evident today. The town is the oldest north of Tucson.

In 1863, Henry Wickenburg discovered the Vulture Mine, which in time became the richest gold mine in Arizona's history. In the early 1900s, as the mine played out, ranching and tourism took over as economic mainstay in the area. Wickenburg was incorporated in 1909.

Today, Wickenburg offers a relaxing western life style with a full range of municipal and private sector services.

Traditionally, tourism, cattle ranching, and agriculture have been the main economic activities in Wickenburg. There has also been a small amount of gold mining still in the area. In 1964, Wickenburg began to diversify its economic base by devel-

144

oping an industrial airpark to encourage manufacturing firms to locate in the town.

Judy Luna's Story

The interview with Judy took place at her home. Judy is a 58 year old widow. She has lived in Wickenburg for 31 years. Originally she and her husband, Raphael, lived in the southernmost area of the state, in the town of Nogales. There they owned a small furniture business importing furniture from old Mexico. Judy sold their business in 1965 after Raphael suffered a fatal heart attack. Left with a young son and a keen business sense, she decided to relocate to central Arizona to the town of Wickenburg and open a Mexican restaurant.

Judy bought her current home in 1966. Judy chose not to remarry. Her only son, who visits her regularly, now lives close by. Judy's experience with ghostly hauntings have all taken place in her home and have indeed given her some very frightful moments. Her following story will offer some eerie proof of the existence of life after death.

There are so many things I can tell you about this house and my experiences, I just don't know where to begin. Both my son and I have seen the ghost of a woman appear to us during the day and night. Even a few neighbors and visitors to our house have seen the ghost's tell-tale signs. You can bet these experiences left them scared out of their wits! I guess the best place to start my story is when we moved into the house.

When I bought the house 31 years ago, it was in need of many repairs. Even though I knew I would have to invest quite a bit of money to do the necessary repairs, I fell in love with the house as soon as I laid eyes on it. Without the help and support from my friends and family who drove from Nogales to help, it would have been impossible for me to make the move.

145

My brother and father helped with the major repairs on the house, and when they felt I was able to tackle the remainder of the minor fix-ups, they returned to Nogales. My neighbors were very helpful throughout my first year with their advice about which local plumbers and electricians to use. They recommended a very wonderful man originally from Mexico who lived in Wickenburg. He was an expert in building and repairing stone walls. I knew I had made a good decision to move to Wickenburg. However, it was not long before strange things began to happen in the house that caused me to question this decision.

The first ghostly incident took place one evening in the kitchen. My son and I were sitting at the table finishing our dinner. At the time of this incident, I was a smoker. I got the urge to smoke a cigarette, so I reached for my purse.

I pulled a cigarette out of the pack, got up out of my chair, and walked to the pantry where I kept the box of match sticks. Placing the cigarette in my mouth, I turned the match box on its side and carefully took hold of the match. I dragged it against the striking surface of the box. There was a spark as the match was lit. As I raised the lit match to my cigarette, suddenly the lit match left my fingers and sailed across the kitchen! It hovered above the kitchen table for about five seconds before coming down and landing between my son's legs!

It all happened very fast, and I was left with my mouth wide open. My son yelled with pain as the match burned his leg. I quickly came to my senses and rushed to him. Thankfully, he was not badly burned, but was startled nonetheless. I knew that this was not something normal. I had no explanation for how this could have happened without someone or something ghostly being involved.

After this, strange things began to happen on a regular basis. It was as if the match incident was an announcement of things to come. More such experiences took place. I was not willing

146

to admit to myself that my house was haunted, but in a very short time I changed my mind.

One night I was awakened by the sound of noise coming from the living room. I got out of bed and in the darkness, I fumbled and made my way to the living room. I was quite awake when I looked in the direction of the fireplace. There I saw the image of a woman kneeling at the fireplace opening. She turned her attention to me and then stood up. She was a small woman who was dressed in a long brown dress. Standing, she faced me and slowly began to fade until she was gone. That's when the emotion of fear really gripped me. I turned on every light in the house!

Weeks passed after this last incident before another strange occurrence took place. One morning at about eleven, I was walking from the bedroom to the living room. Suddenly an orange-yellow light came flying right past my left side. It appeared to come from the bedroom I had just came from. It was a dull light; the color was like the light that a low wattage yellow bulb would cast. It moved right by me, and as I followed it with my eyes, it moved quickly down the hallway to the living room where it disappeared! Of course, I had no explanation for this. My son, who was watching cartoons in the living room, also witnessed the light and screamed. I ran to my son and comforted him. Not wishing to alarm him any further, I reassured him that it was nothing to be concerned about. My own thoughts were, however, quite different.

After this last incident, we both began to see more examples of ghostly lights. Once as my son and I were seated at the kitchen table having dinner, we both saw what I can only describe as a dancing spark appear on top of a family picture which was hung on the living room wall. The spark moved up and down around the framed picture, then leaped to the coffee table. It then flew up into the air and made two large tracing circles about the room before it disappeared. We were amazed at the spectacular light show and unable to find a cause for such a display.

Another afternoon, I was entertaining some neighbors I had invited for lunch. We were all seated around the kitchen table talking. A neighbor named Cecilia asked me if I was aware of the strange lights in my house. She informed me that glowing lights were seen on several occasions by some of the neighbors. At the time that these lights were witnessed in the house, it was unoccupied.

Cecilia described the lights as "darting from room to room." Soon a rumor got around town that the house was haunted. Cecilia also told me about the original builders of the house, and the tragic history of the woman who once lived here with her family.

One cold winter morning, the woman was placing wood into the fireplace and apparently got too close to the fire; her dress was ignited. Instead of immediately wrapping herself in a blanket or other covering to smother the flames, she ran screaming throughout the house. This action only fueled the flames to burn hotter and faster. Eventually, hearing the screams, her husband caught up to her and put out the fire. Although he did the best he could, it was obvious that his help came too late. The woman suffered a lot of serious burns on her body and face. She was taken to a hospital in Phoenix, many miles away. He had to locate a car for transportation and then make the long drive to Phoenix, which at that time took most of the day. Due to the woman's loss of skin and severe shock, she died a few days after her arrival at the hospital.

After hearing the story of the burned woman, I decided to keep my own experiences with the ghost woman a secret. I did not want to draw any more attention to my house. This new information provided the explanation I needed to clear up unanswered questions. It must have been a very painful and drawn out death for that woman. I can't begin to imagine what it would have been like to experience such a horror. Luckily, my son was not present to hear the neighbor's story.

My response to the neighbors was only to say, "Well, I haven't experienced anything like that at all since I've been here. Perhaps the lights everyone saw were caused by some kids playing with flashlights."

The only thing I felt I could do to get rid of any future hauntings would be to pray and seek the help of our local priest. The priest offered to bless the house, and nothing unusual happened during the blessing, just the usual holy water, prayers, and incense. After the house blessing I purchased a small picture of Saint Joan de Arch. I believe that due to the fact that this particular saint was put to death by fire, she might help in my situation.

I placed the picture of the saint on top of the fireplace mantle, and next to it a glass of water which to me, symbolizes the power to put-out fires, along with any negative spiritual forces. I'm glad to report that after all these years, my son and I have not been visited by any more ghosts or lights. I hope everything stays that way from now on.

WINSLOW

Winslow, which became a division point for the Santa Fe Railway, lies along Interstate 40 on the western border of Navajo County in the high plateau country of northeastern Arizona.

The community, at an elevation of 4,850 feet, lies in the Little Colorado River Valley, the river that skirts the city's eastern edge, 58 miles east of Flagstaff. Famed Route 66 was the major east-west route through Winslow before I-40 replaced it.

The first settler, in 1880, was reputed to have been a hotel man who lived in and did business from a tent. Two years later, in January 1882, a U.S. Post Office was established. Incorporated in 1900, the town was said to have been named for Edward Winslow, a railroad company president. However, Tom Winslow, a prospector and early resident, claimed the settlement was named for him.

Today, Winslow has a diversified economy; transportation, tourism, manufacturing, trade and retail business are important factors. The Santa Fe Railway and the Arizona Department of Corrections are the major employers with 500 employees each. Trade is the second largest employer, partly due to tourism brought in by traffic on I-40 and state Highway 87, which con-

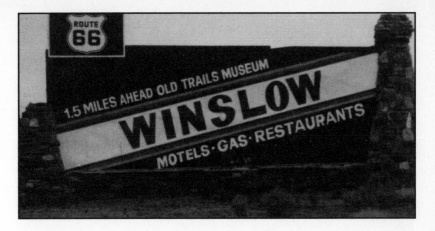

nects Winslow to Phoenix. State Highway 87 continues north into the Navajo and Hopi Indian reservations.

Georgiana Chambers' Story

My interview with Georgiana was conducted in the kitchen of the home of Georgiana's daughter, Doreen. As Georgiana and I readied ourselves for the interview, Doreen was busy at the other end of the table feeding her granddaughter an afternoon meal. I could not help but notice that Georgiana is a short woman, perhaps around 5'3". My attention was also drawn to her strong liking for silver and turquoise jewelry. Geogiana wore two bracelets on her left wrist, three rings on her right hand, and four rings on her left. She apparently also enjoyed the habit of smoking cigarettes, as throughout the interview no sooner had she finished smoking one, another was quickly lit with the remaining ember of the last.

Georgiana wasted no time in telling her story of what happened to her and her family while living in the town of Winslow. Here is her story.

I don't mind telling you that I am 64 years old. When the ghost began to appear to me and my family, I must have been

"Mother would dream of having such a comfortable home."

about 12 or 13. My family moved to Arizona when I was just a baby. We settled in Winslow from the New Mexico town of Gallup. We never thought about witches or ghosts or any other weird things like that. We pretty much thought such rumors and talk was all "bunk." About the only people who mentioned ghosts were the Navajos that lived north of town.

Next to our home and property stood another home which was owned by a husband and wife, James and Billie Mae Wakeman. This couple lived by themselves, as they did not have any children of their own. They had to be in their late 60s because they both had grey hair, and Mr. Wakeman walked with a cane. They had a beautiful old house. The garden was always filled with gorgeous zinnias and huge sunflowers, which Billie Mae was so proud of. My brother and I were always hanging around the garden trying to capture the butterflies that were attracted to the brightly-colored flowers. Mrs. Wakeman didn't care how long we spent at her house; I think she and Mr. Wakeman enjoyed having us children around.

Several times the Wakemans invited our family over to dinner. My mother was always impressed by how spotless they kept their home. Naturally, not having to pick up after children was the main reason. Since our family rented the house we lived in, it was always a dream of ours to actually own our own house. My mother dreamed about having such a comfortable home as the Wakemans.

The garden was always filled with gorgeous zinnias and huge sunflowers which Billie Mae was so proud of.

Another dream my mother had was to have such beautiful hair as Mrs. Wakeman's. Mrs. Wakeman's hair was naturally curly, and she always wore it loose. Once I overheard a conversation that my mother and she had about hair care. Mrs. Wakeman informed my mother, "You know, the best thing for hair is rainwater. I have a metal rain barrel right outside the back door where I catch the rain off the roof and use it to rinse my hair. It's wonderful. I also like to add just a small amount of vinegar with the last rinse." Being a young teenager, I was fascinated. Although I never tried it myself, it sure did sound like a wonderful beauty tip at the time.

One March afternoon on Palm Sunday the following year, my family and I returned from church service. The year was 1921. I was in my room about to remove my church clothes when there was a knock at our front door. It was Mr. Wakeman. I remember he was very upset and in a anxious voice said to my parents, "Please, you have to come and help me. Billie Mae fell, and I can't wake her." We all rushed to their house and there on the kitchen floor we found Mrs. Wakeman. My mother and I began to cry. I was so scared. I had never seen anyone in such a condition before.

The doctor was immediately called and after he examined Mrs. Wakeman, he sadly informed Mr. Wakeman that Mrs. Wakeman had suffered a heart attack and was dead. It was such a terrible surprise to us all. Mr. Wakeman was devastated. They had spent so many years together, and now it was all over. He never fully recovered from his wife's death. As the months went by we noticed that he became weaker, and eventually he decided to move to the southern city of Phoenix. His younger sister lived in Phoenix with her own family and she decided that he would be better cared for living with them.

One day Mr. Wakeman invited my mother and father to his home and asked them if they would be interested in purchasing his house. My parents were surprised but wasted no time in responding. Soon we moved from our rented home and into the Wakeman's. We now had a home of our own with a garden of flowers for my very own! Understand that we were all very sad to have gotten a house through such a sad turn of events, but the opportunity was given to us, and we were happy.

As the months passed, I recall a cold November night when I was asked by my father to go outside to the woodpile at the rear of the house. It was a cold night, and the fire in the wood stove needed to be fueled. I bundled up, and, with an old blanket to place the wood in, I went outside. I laid the blanket on the ground and began to stack the wood in a neat pile within the center.

Suddenly, I heard my name being called. I stopped my work and looked around. I didn't see anyone. Thinking it was my mother, I walked back into the house and asked who had called me. My mother said, "You're hearing things, Georgiana. Hurry up, now, I need that wood or else we're all going to freeze." Back to the wood pile I returned. I knew my name had been called out. I was sure of it.

I began to stack the wood on the blanket as before. Then I heard, "Georgiana, what are you doing, my dear?" I immediately stopped what I was doing, looked up, and saw Mrs. Wakeman!

I was so scared and wanted to run, but her ghost was standing in front of the path that led to the house. I began to shake so much that I guess her ghost could sense my fright. Her ghost smiled a warm and loving big smile. Although it was a dark night, I could clearly see her beautiful grey hair. Then, once again I heard her say in a whispering voice, "Dear, I'm alright. James is also going to be fine." My body stopped shaking, and it was then that I became aware of the tears that were falling from my eyes. As Mrs. Wakeman's ghost slowly disappeared, deep within me I felt a feeling of both sadness and happiness.

I returned to the house, and as I entered the living room, my mother came running to my side asking, "What happened, baby? What's wrong?" I was unable to control myself. I hugged my mother and cried out, "I saw her, Mother. Mrs. Wakeman appeared to me!" After a few minutes of consoling from both my parents, I explained to them what I had seen.

Although it was difficult for my mother and father to accept my story, they could not brush away the effect it obviously had on me. We all agreed to not mention to anyone what I had seen. Two days later, we received a letter from Mr. Wakeman's sister. She wrote that Mr. Wakeman had physically taken a turn for the worse and died in his sleep. My family was surprised by the news, but I was more than surprised. The reassuring words Mrs. Wakeman's ghost had spoken to me two nights before about her beloved husband, "James is going to be fine," now made sense to me. Her spirit had trusted me enough to give me the news about his death.

It was not long after the visit of Mrs. Wakeman's ghost that night that strange things started to happen in our house. Even my father was a witness to this.

At around 11 pm one night, we were all asleep in bed when we were awakened by the sound of noise in the kitchen. The noise was the sound that dishes make hitting against each other. Immediately, I thought that someone had broken into our home and was robbing us. I watched from the safety of my bedroom door as my father cautiously entered the kitchen. He was just a few feet away from the doorway when he suddenly let out a yell; "Get out of our house. You're dead. Please go. Leave now!" My father had seen the same ghost of Mrs. Wakeman that I had seen just a few nights before in our backyard. Although I did not personally see the ghost this time, my father's nervous reaction told the whole story. My father never explained to my brother and me what he had seen that frightened him so much that night. However, I did speak to my mother when my father was not around, and she told me what father witnessed.

It was just as I had thought. Standing in the kitchen that night was the ghost of Mrs. Wakeman. Father became a believer in ghosts that night and has since chosen not to discuss any such topic relating to the supernatural.

Since the years following the last ghostly visit from Mrs. Wakeman, we had not seen or heard any more ghosts. My parents eventually sold the house to a couple from California who lived in it for a while, until it became too much to maintain and repair. One day it was torn down, and the land it stood on was left vacant for many years. I understand from the folks in the neighborhood that no improvements have been made to the property. One of these days, when I'm able to, I'd like to return to that old property and plant a couple of sunflower seeds in the ground. It would be nice to see flowers growing in Bille Mae's garden once again. I think she would be happy if I did that.

YUMA

Yuma is in the far southwest corner of Arizona, just below where the Colorado and Gila Rivers converge. Since prehistoric times, Yuma has been the best site for crossing the Colorado River. Yuma was named for the Yuman Indians, so called because of their habit of setting fires along the river (*humo* meaning smoke in Spanish). Fort Yuman was built during the

gold rush to establish an Anglo presence in the area and to ensure a southern route into California.

First established in 1854 as Colorado City, the town became Arizona City and finally Yuma. Incorporated under the name Arizona City in 1871, it was reincorporated as Yuma in 1873 and now serves as the Yuma County seat. At an elevation of 138 feet, Yuma remains a day crossroad for air and land transportation, although steamboats no longer carry supplies to mining communities and forts "up river."

Agriculture plays a dominant role in the Yuma County economy. Tourist business, composed mainly of cross-country travelers and winter visitors, creates an estimated gross revenue of $368.8 million.

History of the Yuma County Courthouse

Built during 1928 according to the design of San Diego architects Ralph Swearingen and G .A. Hanssen, the third Yuma County Courthouse is a good local example of the Second Renaissance Revival style. The building was erected at a cost of more than $100,000 to replace a similar facility on the same site destroyed by fire on August 18, 1927. As the seat of Yuma County since 1928, the Courthouse has acquired additional significance as a symbol of government and as a distinctive landmark within the community.

History of the ghost of the Yuma County Courthouse

Within the apparent safety of stone and concrete walls of the courthouse, are employees who have their own, very different story of a ghost whom they identify as being that of a former bailiff, Adolph Teichman. Mr. Teichman worked and lived in a loft above the second floor of the courthouse. He died on Christmas morning, 1949, at 82 years of age. In life, Mr. Teichman measured 5' 7", was hunched over, and was known to walk with a peculiar shuffling gate. His demeanor was quiet and friendly. City clerks who worked—and still work—the evening hours have witnessed an elderly, hunched man who walks the hallways in a shuffling manner. Could this be the loyal employee of the court house who now refuses to leave his former home?

Mr. Teichman is buried in Yuma at the northeast corner of Desert Lawn Memorial Park, next to his brother. There is no headstone to mark the resting place for either brother. Perhaps, Mr. Teichman would now very much welcome a small token of appreciation from the citizens of Yuma. A small headstone perhaps? After all—death or no death—he still is very devoted to serving as caretaker of the court house. Just ask anyone who has worked during the late night hours on the second and third floors. He's around all right, still keeping a watchful eye on "his" courthouse.

Cecil J. Roach's Story

My interview with Cecil took place in the maintenance office, located in the basement of the courthouse. During the interview, Cecil nervously chuckled and wrung his hands as he related his experiences. He was quite aware of the skepticism and perplexed

Cecil J. Roach

attitude people who have never experienced a ghost for themselves, might have towards his story. Undaunted by this, he presented a

*straightforward and focused account of what he believes to be behind
the unusual activity that begins in the courthouse, after the light of day
disappears.*

As the maintenance foreman, I have been working at the
courthouse for five years. Prior to working at the courthouse, I
don't recall any stories of ghost or hauntings being told to me.
However, once employed and well into my job, certain individuals did feel comfortable enough with my personality to
open up and tell me about their own stories and experiences.
Of course, I thought that behind these stories was another purpose. I thought people just wanted to have fun with me and get
a good laugh.

Some stories that the secretaries have told me about their
own experiences were about refusing to work in the evening
hours because they see the ghost of an old man dressed in a
suit. They say that the ghost resembles the photos of the dead
caretaker, Adolph Teichman, who walks the halls. Doors will
open and slam on their own. Also I've heard talk of file cards
flying across the rooms while the secretaries are busy at their
computers. They also hear footsteps and sometimes will even
be touched on the shoulders. These things don't always happen just during the night hours. In the basement, during the
day workers have heard voices of laughter coming from empty
rooms.

Assistants who work with me have told me about seeing the
same old man who walks down the hall and then gradually disappears. One assistant came to me one early morning yelling,
"Cecil, Cecil, there's a bum loose in the courthouse!" He
explained that as he looked through one of the glass windows
built into an office door, he saw an old man moving about the
room. The assistant attempted to open the door and confront
the old guy, but it was locked. He described the man as being
about 80 years old and wearing an old, worn suit. Another

assistant told me about an old man who walked right past him, brushing him on the side in the hallway. When the worker turned to see where the old man was headed, he simply was no longer there. He just disappeared into thin air!

There also was an instance when one of the office service bells had, we thought, been stolen. It was missing for over a year, then recently workers began to hear the sound of the ringing bell coming from the office. Maintenance workers informed me of hearing a ringing bell coming from that same office at 6 am. Of course, we looked and didn't see a bell, but just a few hours later, a secretary came to me holding the missing bell! She said that she found it in the office and had no idea how it had reappeared after being missing for so long. I was strange to me was why that darn bell was ringing on its own in an empty office at 6 am! It wasn't until I had my own first experience with the ghost that I began to slowly understand that I was working in a haunted building.

My shift always began at 3 am I was given the responsibility of carrying the master key of the courthouse, and with that responsibility, I had to be sure to lock the doors behind me. Once in the courthouse I turned on the lights. I was always the only person in the building.

One night, 10 months into my job, I began to hear noises and footsteps of someone walking up and down the second floor hallway and slamming doors. I was on the first floor, and I recall going right up the stairs to see who was making all the noise. I looked all around and called out, "Is anyone here?" There was no response and no one in sight. This went on off and on for a few nights, then the noises stopped.

About a year later at, 4 am I was once again alone in the building. I was buffing the hallway with a buffing machine, and over the soft humming sound of the machine, I began to hear the sound of someone whistling. I stopped the machine and listened to the fading whistle sound as it disappeared down the hall. I started up the machine once more. Again, the whistling began. I turned off the machine and walked up the hallway opening each office door and looking inside to see if I could catch anyone. The place was empty. Because I didn't see anyone in the flesh, I somehow got the courage to return to finishing up my job. I returned to buffing the floor. The whistling started up again, only this time it was right behind me! Yeah, I was concerned, maybe even a little scared.

After that odd experience, I had others. Sometimes when I'm working, I like to have my radio playing in the hallway to keep me company. The music also helps to keep me active in the early hours. As soon as I would leave the hallway or room, it would shut off on its own! I thought perhaps there was an electrical problem with the outlet or even with the radio itself. As I returned to where I placed the radio, I noticed that the radio's electrical cord was lying on the floor, disconnected from the wall! Now, this might sound strange, and it might appear to be a problem with a certain wall outlet, but even stranger was that this happened on every floor and wall outlet I plugged the radio into.

My choice of music was not the only thing that the ghost did not like. My coffee maker was also unplugged. Sometimes I brought my coffee maker with me and plugged it into a wall where I was working. When I returned to see if the coffee was done brewing, I discovered that the cord was pulled from the wall, just like my radio. One time I returned to find the extension cord I had connected the coffer maker to was also disconnected and was wrapped around a trash can with one end inside the can! Now, how can anyone explain that?

Soon I began to notice these strange things happening more frequently in the month of December. Even stranger, the activity would intensified as the days got closer to Christmas. One year, at about 5 am, as I was getting out of the elevator on the second floor, a voice loudly called out my name, "Cecil, Cecil!" Of course there was no one in the elevator with me, but I turned around anyway just to be sure. I saw no one. Now, that really scared me and gave me goose bumps.

Just last year, two days before Christmas, I had an assistant helping me in the building. I was on the second floor where the

"As I began to walk pass the door, it opened wide and forcefully!"

courtrooms are located. Suddenly, I saw one of the doors to a courtroom open. Since the courtrooms are to be locked securely due to strict security procedures, I immediately investigated. I entered the courtroom, turned on the lights and looked around cautiously. I saw no one. I locked the door behind me and walked down the hall. I came upon the door which lead up to the top floor where Adolph Teichman used to live. As I began to walk past the door,

it opened wide! When this happened, I moved so fast, I don't even remember how I reached the first floor!

Not long after, I was with another assistant when we had a joint experience so frightening that even to this day, I can't get it out of my mind. Again, it took place in the morning hours. We were both seated in my office talking, when suddenly we heard noise coming from the hallway. The noise was of some-one hitting and spinning the lid on a trash can. Thinking that this unusual noise was caused by a security guard who had entered the building, we waited for him to come to my office and pay us a visit. After a few seconds had passed, I got up out of my chair and checked the hallways and doors. The doors were locked, and I assumed that we were the only ones in the building.

We disregarded this latest strange experience and soon got back to work. My assistant climbed the stairs to the third floor, and I remained on the first floor. Everything was going as usual until I heard a noise and then saw something coming down the stairs. You might think I'm crazy, but as I looked to the stairs, I saw a large black ball floating down the stairs, with a smaller black ball following behind! The larger ball was the size of a basketball. The smaller ball also followed the larger ball by about four feet. They were traveling quickly, as quickly as someone running down the stairs might move. As the balls reached the landing, they

"I saw a large black ball floating down the stairs!"

disappeared. I can't explain the thoughts and feelings that went through me. I was shaking and covered in goose bumps. I can't say any more about that night. It was a very frightening thing to witness.

Throughout the years, I have heard and seen lots of things in this building There is definitely something here. I know there is. Because I still work in the courthouse, I would rather not see anymore ghosts or hear whistling, the ringing of bells, or other sounds again! I mean it! I want the ghost to know that I want to be left alone.

Yuma Territorial Prison

On July 1, 1876, the first seven inmates entered the Territorial Prison at Yuma and were locked into the new cells they had built themselves.

A total of 3,069 prisoners, including 29 women, lived within these walls during the prison's 33 years of operation. Their crimes ranged from murder to polygamy, with grand larceny being the most common. A majority served only portions of their sentences due to the

ease with which paroles and pardons were obtained. 111 persons died while serving their sentences, most from tuberculosis, which was common throughout the territory. Of the many prisoners who attempted escape, 26 were successful, but only two were from within the prison confines. No executions took place at the prison because capital punishment was administered by the county government.

Despite an infamous reputation, written evidence indicates that the prison was humanely administered and was a model institution for its time. The only punishments were the dark cell for inmates who broke prison regulations and the ball and chain for those who tried to escape. Prisoners had free time when they hand-crafted many items to be sold at public bazaars held at the prison on Sundays after church services. Prisoners also had regular medical attention and access to a good hospital.

Schooling was available for convicts, and many learned to read and write in prison. The prison housed one of the first "public" libraries in the territory, and visitor's fees for tours of the institution were used to purchase books. One of the early electrical generating plants in the West furnished power for lights and ran a ventilation system in the cell block.

By 1907, the prison was severely overcrowded, and there was no room on Prison Hill for expansion. The convicts constructed a new facility in Florence, Arizona. The last prisoner left Yuma on September 15, 1909.

The Yuma Union High School occupied the buildings from 1910 to 1914. Empty cells provided free lodging for hobos riding the freights in the 1920s and later sheltered many homeless families during the Depression. Townspeople considered the complex a source for free building material. This, plus fires, weathering, and railroad construction, destroyed the prison walls and all buildings except the cells, main gate and guard tower, but today these provide a glimpse of convict life a century ago.

Linda D. Offeney's Story

My present position at the prison is as Park Ranger 2. My duties requires me to be the curator, tour guide, and front desk clerk. I've worked at the prison as a ranger for over 14 years and have lived in Yuma for a total of 18 years.

Before working here, I never gave the matter of ghosts much thought. Now, my thoughts have changed, because I can't explain the strange things that we all have witnessed.

One night, alone in the facility, I began my usual

Linda D. Offeney

evening security check of the prison grounds. Walking outside the museum, I made my way toward an area of the prison known as the dark cell. Years ago, when the prison was in use, this particular cell was used as punishment for those prisoners who were not following the rules. It was solitary confinement. The dark cell to this very day is not a very pleasant area to visit. As the name implies, it is dark and very eerie.

As I continued my security check, I walked over to the dark cell and proceeded to check the iron gate located at its entrance. Suddenly, I felt the presence of someone gazing at me from within the cell. I was overcome with a feeling of fear. I had made the same check many times before, but this time something was different. This time, the hair on the back of my neck stood on end. I didn't actually see anything, but I sure did feel the horrible gaze of something staring back at me. I quickly made sure that the gate was locked and hurried away from that area. Returning to the comfort and safety of the museum, I thought about what had transpired and just could not shake the feeling of those eyes staring at me.

As a point of information, in our files is a picture that was taken in the late 1930s of a woman standing by the cell block area where the dark cell is located. The woman is not the ghost, but in the background behind her is the figure of a ghostly man. He appears to be outfitted in a World War I uniform. The soldier is standing in the archway to the left of the opening to the dark cell. The rangers who have seen the picture think that this room—which is now walled up—is where the insane prisoners were kept until they were transferred to an outside asylum. The woman is apparently unaware of the ghost standing just a few feet away behind her.

Another strange occurrence at the prison is when visitors report to me that they have been pinched while in the dark cell. I began to notice a pattern that these guests all shared; they all wore clothing of which the dominant color was red. It made no difference if they were in the company of others or by themselves. They got pinched! Keep in mind that these were visitors who were unrelated and came to my desk at different times of the year. I can't explain it.

Another day, I took a tour of children into the dark cell. I gathered them all around and told them the history of the cell and, not wanting to frighten them, I kept the information as much as possible on a pleasant level. Well, in the middle of the tour I had a child who was wearing red clothing state to me and the group that someone had just pinched her! I tactfully ended my talk and escorted the children out the door.

Three years ago we had a visiting staff writer from *Arizona Highways* magazine pay us a visit. She wanted to do a story about the prison and got the strange idea of spending two days and nights in the dark cell—alone. She wished to "experience" the isolation that a prisoner might have had in years gone by. She even asked to be chained by her foot to the cell, as a prisoner would have been. We provided her with a jug of water and loaf of white bread and placed a heavy blanket over the entrance to the cell to keep out any sunlight. We also provided her with a makeshift toilet, which brought a smile to her face.

She had anticipated to remain in the dark cell much longer than she did, but she soon discovered that she was not welcomed. As she described it, she began to sense the presence of someone else in the cell with her. She began to feel pinching or prickling sensations all over her body. We soon heard her alerted calls to us to get her out of the cell quickly, which we did.

Before I end my story, I do want to tell you about a unusual character that dwells inside the museum, whom we all refer to as "Johnny." There were evenings when I was at the cash register totaling up the day's money. A strange thing happened. As I had the register drawer open, suddenly, the coins jumped out! It was as if an invisible finger was flicking the coins out of the drawer compartments.

There were also other times when I was standing over the opened cash drawer with a hand full of coins. The coins suddenly jumped out of my hand and into the drawer! Now, is that strange or what! Other staff workers have also seen this happen. "Johnny" does not seem to be interested in paper money, just coins. We don't know who this playful ghost is, or why he is so interested in money. He still performs his antics every now and then with us.

There are other unusual things that happen here. The local people in town have reported to us that they see lights from oil lanterns moving about the prison in the evening hours when it is closed. These lights have always been seen in the cell block area of the prison. We have visitors and staff who have reported incidences of hearing voices of men in low conversation. These are usually heard in the museum area.

My own personal attitude about ghosts in the prison is that they will not hurt me. I just know they won't. More of a concern to me is encountering a rattlesnake or skunk that might have decided to venture into the facility. We have had such unwelcome visitors in the past. However, if I were to actually see a ghost of one of the prisoners, I

In memory of the inmates, who lost their life while serving their sentence, at the Arizona territorial prison at Yuma. Of the 3,069 convicts sentenced to Yuma prison 111 met their death. Disease, accident, murder, suicide, and escape attempts were the causes of their demise. The remains of 104 unfortunate souls are interred in this cemetery.

would like to sit down and ask him a question or two about his experiences. I know it would scare me to death, but I would still be interested.

Jesse M. Torres' Story

Currently, I am the assistant park manager and have been employed at the prison for over 16 years. I was born and raised in Yuma, and because the prison is so familiar, I didn't really think much about it as a historic site. Little did I know that one day I would be responsible for its well-being.

Before working at the prison, I heard stories in town about the place being

Jesse M. Torres, in front of cell #7

haunted. I'm basically a skeptic, so I didn't pay these stories any mind. I used to think that if I ever felt or heard anything which might be paranormal, it had to be my imagination. That's what I *used* to think.

My first experience with ghosts at the prison took place when I was about 8 years old. I was brought to the prison during a school field trip. As the school group was led through the grounds by our teacher, we passed an area of the prison named the "New Yard." The group was walking ahead of me as I lingered in front of cell number 7. Something drew me to this cell, and as I looked inside, I saw a man dressed in a striped prisoner uniform standing inside the closed iron door. At the time, I felt uneasy and quickly ran to keep up with my classmates.

171

The museum staff has had visitors tell us that they have also seen a prisoner in that very same cell, dressed in prison striped clothes!

Eight years after I began working at the prison, I had an experience I will never forget. The current storage room in the museum used to be used as an office by the staff. One day, as I was in the museum cleaning the glass cases that hold artifacts of daily prison life, I heard voices coming from the office. Knowing I was alone in the building, I stood still and listened. The voices were soft whispers of men in conversation. I clearly heard one or two words that I recognized, but I was unable to make a complete sentence out of them. Thinking that some unauthorized person was in the building, I quietly walked to the office door, took hold of the door knob, and opened the door. Once I turned on the light, I saw that the room was completely empty; the voices I had just heard a few seconds ago were now gone.

Another early morning, alone in the museum, I clearly heard a voice demand, "Jesse, did you get it?" Startled by such a request, I turned around to face the person. I saw no one. I felt the hair on my neck stand right up!

Another experience in the prison took place in the old cell block, directly outside cell number 14. One winter day, as I was walking down the cell bock area, I walked past cell number 14. A movement in the cell caught my eye, and as I looked through the spaces of the iron door, I saw a white-colored figure moving about

Outside Cell #14

172

inside! Other staff members have also see this figure, and have heard its footsteps as it moves about the cell. Visitors who know nothing about the history of cell number 14 have approached us to say that they have heard a noise and have felt the "heavy presence" of someone in the cell.

From old prison records, I discovered some information about a prisoner named John Ryan. As listed on the prison records, his was a "crime against nature." In early prison history, "crime against nature" was a label given to prisoners who had committed rape or other such sexual deviations. The records also showed that Mr. Ryan did not get along well with the other prisoners and was placed alone in cell number 14! While in the cell, he committed suicide by hanging himself with a rope made from his blankets.

John Ryan

Description of Convict

Name: John Ryan   Number: 1660
Crime: Crime against nature Sentence: 5 yrs. from 9/28/1900
County: Coconino   Nativity: Iowa
Legitimate Occupation: Miner-Cooking   Age: 31
Habits: Intemperate   Tobacco: Yes
Opium: No   Religion: Catholic
Size of Head: 7 1/8   Size of Foot: 8
Color of Eyes: Gray   Color of Hair: Light Brown
Married: Yes   Children: 3

Can Read: Yes Can Write: Yes
Where Educated: Iowa
When and How Discharged: May 6, 1903 Committed Suicide
by hanging in cell about 11:30 a.m.

PRISON RECORD
NOV. 10, 1900: SOLITARY 3 DAYS FOR FIGHTING.
MAR. 12, 1901: SOLITARY 11 DAYS FOR STRIKING
A FELLOW CONVICT.
MAY 27, 1902: SOLITARY 4 DAYS FOR INSUBOR-
DINATION.

SUPT.'S REPORT, MAR. 31, 1901- REPORT ABOUT
HIS BEING TEMPORARILY DEMENTED

In another area of the prison is a cell named the dark cell.
The staff has had several visitors relate to us that when in the
dark cell, an unseen entity—or ghost—pinches them. Some
visitors feel such a negative presence that they have refused to
enter the room during our ranger-guided tours. Once, a man
stated that while visiting the dark cell, he saw moving and
flashing lights. He said he was not about to stay in there
another moment and quickly left.

When it was in use, the dark cell was a form of punishment
to any prisoner who fought, was caught stealing, or tried to riot.
Within the dark cell was a large iron cage with two iron rings
at opposite corners. First, the prisoner was stripped down to his
underwear. Next, the prisoner's legs were chained—one leg to
each iron ring. His only food was plain bread and water. The
prison records do not mention any prisoner ever dying while in
the dark cell, but the records do state that at least two prisoners did leave the dark cell, only to be immediately transferred
to an insane asylum in Phoenix.

I think that there are spirits trapped in the walls of the

prison. But I find it strange that the prison cemetery lacks any ghost activity. One would think that of all places on the grounds to be haunted, it would have to be the cemetery. I don't go in for such stuff as ghosts or hauntings, but what we have seen here does cause me to wonder.

The End

FINIS CORONAT.

Other Books
by Antonio R. Garcez

Adobe Angels -
The Ghosts of Las Cruces and Southern New Mexico
Published 1996
ISBN 0-9634029-4-3

Adobe Angels -
The Ghosts of Santa Fe and Taos
Revised 1995
ISBN 0-9634029-3-5

Adobe Angels -
The Ghosts of Albuquerque
Published 1992
ISBN 0-9634029-2-7

The above titles are available at all bookstores
or by writing directly to :

Red Rabbit Press
P.O. Box 968
Truth or Consequences, NM 87901